"This moment has been a long time in coming."

Strakhov addressed Bolan, but the Executioner was eyeing the pistols trained on him from across the table. He was also aware of the woman's gun barrel, pressed against his neck.

"I, too, have spent the same amount of time waiting for this," Bolan said.

Strakhov considered Bolan's words, then drew himself erect. "Enough! The time has come to end it. I had anticipated pulling the trigger myself, but I think it would be more enjoyable to the high council, as well as being a true test of Miss Yesilov's loyalty, if I ordered her to shoot you. Are you agreeable to that, Agent Yesilov?"

The muzzle of the Walther PPK did not budge from Bolan's nape. "I am," the blonde replied.

"Then kill him," Strakhov snarled. "I want to see the Executioner die."

Tanya Yesilov squeezed the trigger.

MACK BOLAN

The Executioner

DON PENDLETON's EXECUTIONER

MACK BOLAN

Moscow Massacre

A GOLD EAGLE BOOK FROM

W♦RLDWIDE

TORONTO • NEW YORK • LONDON • PARIS
AMSTERDAM • STOCKHOLM • HAMBURG
ATHENS • MILAN • TOKYO • SYDNEY

First edition August 1986

ISBN 0-373-61092-0

Special thanks and acknowledgment to
Stephen Mertz for his contributions to this work.

Printed in Canada

Dedicated to the sixty dead, victims of the hijacked Egyptian Boeing 737 at Luqa Airport, Malta, November 1985.

THE
MACK BOLAN
LEGEND

Nothing less than a war could have fashioned the destiny of the man called Mack Bolan. Bolan earned the Executioner title in the jungle hellgrounds of Vietnam, for his skills as a crack sniper in pursuit of the enemy.

But this supreme soldier also wore another name—Sergeant Mercy. He was so tagged because of the compassion he showed to wounded comrades-in-arms and Vietnamese civilians.

Mack Bolan's second tour of duty ended prematurely when he was given emergency leave to return home and bury his family. Bolan made his peace at his parents' and sister's gravesite. Then he declared war on the evil force that had snatched his loved ones. The Mafia.

In a fiery one-man assault, he confronted the Mob head-on, carrying a cleansing flame to the urban menace. And when the battle smoke cleared, a solitary figure walked away alive.

He continued his lone-wolf struggle, and soon a hope of victory began to appear. But Mack Bolan had broken society's every rule. That same society started gunning for this elusive warrior—to no avail.

So Bolan was offered amnesty to work within the system against international terrorism. This time, as an official employee of Uncle Sam, Bolan wore yet another handle: Colonel John Phoenix. With government sanction now, and a command center at Stony Man Farm in Virginia's Blue Ridge Mountains, he and his new allies—Able Team and Phoenix Force—waged relentless war on a new adversary: the KGB and all it stood for.

Until the inevitable occurred. Bolan's one true love, the brilliant and beautiful April Rose, died at the hands of the Soviet terror machine.

Embittered and utterly saddened by this feral deed, Bolan broke the shackles of Establishment authority.

Now the big justice fighter is once more free to haunt the treacherous alleys of the shadow world.

PROLOGUE

It was no place for death.

Myriad twinkling stars encrusted the endless night sky that surveyed the rolling, forested wilderness of the Stony Man Mountain region of rural Virginia, eighty air miles south of Washington, D.C. The darkness was muted by a natural peacefulness, broken only by an occasional nocturnal birdsong and the incessant crackle of night insects.

This was a place for life, not death.

The big man who stood motionless, pensive, in the gloom carried death with him. He had faced the Grim Reaper many times and had always walked away from him. But there were others, friends and foes alike, who had not been so lucky on the hellfire trail. And the aura of mankind's common denominator seemed to follow this man everywhere, clinging, a tangible thing.

Mack Bolan knew it would be so until his turn came.

He had been standing for the past ten minutes, staring down at a simple headstone in the center of a grassy clearing bordered by hardwoods and conifers.

Not a place for death.

And yet Bolan felt strangely comfortable with the knowledge that the dead one, buried beneath this simple marker, rested forever amid pastoral beauty and quiet.

Her name had been April Rose.

She had been the love of Bolan's life.

She had died violently in his arms from a bullet meant for him.

Bolan had killed her slayer in the heartbeat following her death, but it meant nothing now.

Increasingly there were only two things that mattered anymore to a man who had waded mile after mile down Blood River against seemingly impossible odds for all of his adult life.

Two things mattered: the emptiness at the center of his being left by the passing of the woman buried here and the war of attrition he continued to wage—the fighting of a personal war that gave his life meaning. When he thought about what his war had accomplished—the gains made for those who could not fight for themselves—it was the one thing he had left that filled the ever-present ache inside. And Bolan knew that without his kind of help, the good, the meek, would never inherit this savage world.

He wore a dark jacket, sweater and slacks, civilian attire that merged with the shadows of the tree that he stood beneath, indiscernible from the gloom cloaking this scene of a man and his memories.

A shoulder-holstered 9 mm Beretta 93-R nestled beneath the jacket, which remained unbuttoned for fast, easy access.

His thoughts centered on his past and on a spirit that seemed to permeate this place. A spirit that had lived large.

Had lived.

His senses flared at the approach of someone who made no attempt at stealth.

Bolan hit a combat crouch and faded deeper into the murk at the base of the hardwood. His right hand dipped in to palm the butt of the Beretta, unleathering it to fan the night, finally homing on the direction from which a man approached up a starlit incline to the clearing.

Bolan relaxed and reholstered the Beretta when he recognized the stocky figure in a rumpled suit as Hal Brognola. Brognola always appeared uncomfortably out of place away from pavement and offices, like now.

Bolan straightened, materializing out of the shadows.

"Hello, Hal."

Brognola reacted with a small start at those softly spoken words, his first indication of Bolan's presence. Brognola was White House liaison for Stony Man Farm, this well-camouflaged, heavily guarded 160-acre base of operations for the U.S. government's covert antiterrorist operations.

The two men exchanged a firm handshake, and Brognola's grin flashed in the starlight.

"How the hell you do it is beyond me, guy. The security here ranks with the Company site in Langley and the Man himself. How do you do it, Striker?"

It was an old code name from the days when Bolan had taken assignments from Brognola officially.

"I busted those security perimeters, too, Hal, remember? I'm the one who put this operation together."

"You're also the best damn infiltration and combat specialist this country has ever produced," Brognola put in. "It's good to see you, Mack. Been a while since the trial."

Bolan gave Brognola a look that suggested the soldier would rather forget that time. Then he turned toward the grave of the woman he had loved. Still loved.

"You've kept it up real nice, Hal. Thanks."

"Least I could do. She died defending Stony Man Farm that night," Brognola growled. "We take care of our own. Wish we could take care of you. I have the President's ear—"

Bolan had headed the Stony Man operation until not long ago.

"We tried having me play by the rules and it didn't work, Hal," Bolan gently reminded his buddy. Brognola had worked closely with him since the beginning, albeit covertly since Bolan had gone back "into the cold."

Brognola had continued to feed Bolan intel; a top Fed in cahoots with a "vigilante," and only a few highly classified people knew anything about it.

Bolan trusted Brognola all the way.

The Stony Man operation continued its global antiterrorist campaigns via Phoenix Force and Able Team, paramilitary units created by Bolan before he had crossed the line and gone outlaw to find justice in the wake of April Rose's supreme sacrifice.

And justice was at hand now.

It had brought Bolan to this after-midnight rendezvous between two living friends and echoes of a spirit.

"You have what you need," Hal said. "I fed you everything through standard channels. You're risking the whole ballgame coming back here like this."

Bolan's cold blue eyes broke contact with the Fed's gaze, lingering another moment on the unassuming headstone in the clearing. Then he looked at the man from Justice.

"I had to come back. To say goodbye. This one won't be like the others. This one's for the jackpot. When the stakes go that high, anything can happen, even when you've got a handle on it. I had to say goodbye."

Hal's expression softened. "I know, Striker. And I also know what the odds are. Dammit, man, if I could think of any other way to pull this one together—"

"I don't want it any other way, Hal. Strakhov is the target this time. I'd tear myself a piece of this one if you didn't hand it to me."

Hal chuckled without humor. "I know that, too. That's why I asked you in. You'll be taking heavy fire from every side. A headshed hit on KGB headquarters in Moscow. Sure, I can understand you wanting to come back here one more time. The thing between you and Strakhov was born here the night of the attack on the Farm, the night April died."

April had been mission controller and supervisor of the Stony Man operation, centered in the nondescript collection of farmhouses and outbuildings of this "Farm" that camouflaged a sprawling subterranean complex.

Bolan had been the soul of Stony Man Farm.

April had been its heart.

"We should have sized it up from the start," Bolan grunted. "All those terrorist initiatives we fought were connected from the beginning."

Brognola nodded. "That's right. The IRA, the PLO, Armenian extremists. Dozens more, dozens of causes all around the world."

"With one thread connecting them," Bolan finished. "The KGB. And the payback came home to us, and a good woman lies buried here because of it. Strakhov set up that operation—the planting of a deep cover sleeper inside the White House to erode our intelligence services. And they decided to start with a hard hit right here."

"I've gone over it a thousand times in my mind," muttered Brognola. "Maybe we could've done more if you'd stayed on the team, Striker. After you found out who the mole next to the President was and took him out, we could have gone after Strakhov together."

"We are going after him together. And it's my way after all."

"Don't think the irony is lost on many people," Brognola growled. "Okay, guy, you did what you had to do. The Company didn't want that KGB sleeper hit—disinformation potential, all of that—but you took him out anyway. For April, for all of us. I understand that. And I know you well enough to know why you couldn't turn back even when your name went to the top of terminate-on-sight orders for the KGB, the CIA and every other spy agency. You're creating havoc in areas of classified operations with your unsanctioned activities. You declared a one-man war against the KGB for what happened to April, and they and the CIA have declared their own war on you."

"I can't play by the rules anymore, Hal. I was a team member once, and it got April killed. There's an enemy that has to be stopped. The rules don't work. The fact that Strakhov was able to plant a mole at the White House level in the first place is proof enough of that."

Brognola almost took a pace backward at his friend's impassioned outburst. The man from Wonderland knew that Bolan was not given to fiery speeches. For just a heartbeat Brognola wondered if thoughts of revenge were driving the soldier on.

"I just hope they—our side *or* theirs—don't stop you before this operation is over," Hal muttered. "One man, even if he is you, taking on the whole damn KGB! And crippling their operations around the world!" Brognola shook his head as if he still had trouble grasping what Bolan had accomplished since his split from Stony Man. "If I wasn't in on it with you, I'd think the whole thing was unbelievable. Hell, sometimes I think that anyway!"

Bolan knew what Hal meant. He sometimes had trouble himself accepting his longevity in the hellgrounds of the world, from his infantryman days in the Vietnam war through the long bloody years of carrying his one-man war of attrition against the enemy. And, he remembered, they had come in many forms: the Mafia, terrorists and the KGB. While they all had fallen before the vicissitudes of combat, it was far more than luck alone, Bolan knew.

Hal had not exaggerated his estimation of Bolan's capabilities. Bolan had served two tours of Special Forces combat duty in southeast Asia, where he had learned all a man could about guerrilla warfare, commando tactics and staying alive when death came closing in from every flank.

"I've been doing a lot of thinking, Hal. Another reason I wanted to make contact with you before I left the country. It's getting time to shift gears again."

Brognola's expression clouded. "What do you mean?"

"I mean, I've been concentrating most of my time and energies on the KGB."

"And getting some results, to put it mildly. You've been chipping away at the pressure points we could never reach, and there have been plenty of repercussions inside their infrastructure, believe it."

"I'm satisfied with what we've accomplished," Bolan agreed, "but after this headshed hit, if there *is* an after, I think it might be time to broaden the scope even farther."

"What do you have in mind, precisely?"

"I'm not sure. Call it back to the basics, maybe. This old world of ours is going to hell inch by inch everywhere I look, Hal, and the KGB has its grubby hands in most of it, but there are others. The Mafia is getting itself together again. Hell, there's plenty of *un*organized crime stateside, too, that needs going after. I read what's happening to our cities today, and it turns my stomach. There's a lot that needs doing . . . *after* Strakhov."

Strakhov.

Major General Greb Strakhov.

One of the most powerful men commanding the Komitet Gosudarstvennoi Bezopasnosti, the KGB, the global network of death and terror merchants who liked to think of themselves as "The Sword and Shield of the Soviet Union." But, in fact, they represented the muscle, the threat, the knife point held against the throat of civilization by a far-flung militaristic dictatorship that had already gobbled up far too much of the world map.

Bolan had been unable to shake the feeling that it was his duty to do something about the threatening magnitude of the Soviet Union's plans for the world. His "outlaw" campaigns against the hydralike evil responsible for the death of April had already taken him more than once into Russia. And while there he had befriended enough Soviet citizens to reinforce his understanding that the inmates of that sprawling gulag should not be confused with the slave masters in the Kremlin who kept Russians in as cruel a set of shackles as the czars ever had, smothering the spirit of that country, garroting the lives and hopes of its people.

Bolan also recognized that the KGB's activities in the name of socialist expansion had, ironically, a very capitalistic motivation. Countless billions of dollars, he knew, were extorted annually from Soviet-occupied countries and satellites, as well as from the Soviet Union itself, and funneled through a pyramid setup similar to that of the Mafia, with a few boss terrorists like Strakhov fattening their own Swiss bank accounts.

Those billions came from people.

The little people.

The salt of the earth.

The massed hordes of decent, hardworking souls of every country everywhere who wished only to be left alone to live their lives, and maybe find some happiness.

Good people like Bolan's deceased mother, father and sister.

These were the ones for whom Bolan fought.

Mankind mattered to him.

Life mattered.

"I wish I could give you more to go on," Hal said, "but all I've got is enough to get you to Helsinki."

"Rules of the game," Bolan said, nodding. "One thing I would like to know. I still top the TOS list for the CIA and NSA. How high up does the authorization go on this?"

"The top," Hal told him. "The very top."

Bolan grimaced. "I'm not sure if that's good or bad."

"It's the only way it can be. The Chief has always been sympathetic to your situation, Striker, from the beginning, as you know."

"I also know Strakhov had a man next to the Chief."

"Not this time," Brognola assured him. "All I know about this mission is that there's an internal power struggle going on inside the KGB's Moscow headshed even as we speak, and we've got a handle on it—someone on the inside near the top."

"And you don't know who he is, only that he needs help. Only he's not supposed to know I'm helping him. That's a lot of variables, Hal. You know the reason I'm taking on this one."

Hal nodded. "A chance at Strakhov. A chance to rattle their whole damn insides upside down, the way they tried to do when they staged the assault on Stony Man Farm." Brognola paused a beat, then told his friend solemnly, "And I, uh, can see...why you wanted to come back here this one time before you leave the country. The jackpot, like you said."

"For us...or for them," Bolan said, nodding. "Yeah, Hal, I'm in. I wouldn't have it any other way."

"I don't have to tell you they're walking away with the ballgame everywhere the game's in play," Brognola grunted. "They're stealing technology from us like never before. They've pulled the strings to disarm America in the name of peace. Thanks to the Freedom of Information Act, our clandestine operations have been virtually hamstrung by exposure to the world. This is our one chance to turn that whole situation around, and you're our only hope. I'm sending you into the dark, Sarge, but it's the only way we could ensure the secrecy of what you're about to attempt.

"It's going to be the most audacious strike you've ever undertaken. But if this mission is a success, we'll have a man placed at the very top level of the KGB's operation, and you'll have Strakhov in your sights. And that's something everyone wants. That's why this one is being played tighter than ever before. So everyone goes only by what they need to know, and that includes the Man."

"Thanks for bringing me in on it, Hal. My flight leaves from Dulles in ninety minutes."

"Ninety minutes from now?" Brognola said, blinking. "You're going to have to make some damn good time to catch that flight."

"I will. How's Kurtzman?"

"He'll be sorry he missed you and, uh, well, I've taken enough of your time...with April. Good luck, Striker. Watch your back."

They exchanged another warm, firm handshake.

"You watch yours, buddy. There are snakes everywhere," Bolan said.

The Fed turned and disappeared back down the incline the way he had come, the sloping terrain and starry gloom swallowing him up. Bolan turned then and knelt for a brief moment next to the burial marker in the middle of the clearing. Reverently, he touched the chiseled stone script—the name and dates of birth and death, no more—with his fingertips, trying to recall the essence of what he had lost and the spirit that dwelt there. He wished with all the ache in his soul that he could touch the vibrant, alive woman of his memories just one more time.

"This one's for you, April," he whispered in an icy voice to the grave.

Then the big man was one with the night as he straightened abruptly and moved out, away from there.

The blackness devoured him.

WHEN HAL ENTERED the computer room, Aaron "Bear" Kurtzman swung his wheelchair away from the CRT terminal that was spewing green lines of letters and numbers across its display screen.

The walls of the windowless room were lined with consoles housing reels of magnetic tape that revolved in sporadic jabs, the processing units interlocking, reading in and assessing data from countless intel sources around the world.

The surface of the walls and ceiling were specially tiled to dissipate heat as controlled streams of air filtered into the subterranean room to maintain an exact degree of coolness. Uncarpeted floors ensured the absence of unwanted electrical impulses created by static electricity. The man in the wheelchair's protection against the chilled air was his own excess weight, layers of disheveled clothing and a white lab smock.

Kurtzman served as the link between Brognola and the operators running Stony Man Farm's computers. The irascible "Bear" had recovered both mentally and physically from wounds suffered during the KGB-sponsored commando attack on the Farm that had cost the life of April Rose and several members of the security staff; he had fully reconciled himself to the disheartening reality of being wheelchair-bound for life.

The moment Hal dropped into a swivel chair and dug for one of his ever-present stogies, Kurtzman read the Fed's dark expression.

"Let me guess," Kurtzman opened with his usual gruff glint. "*People* magazine has just learned about what we're up to here and wants to do a story on Stony Man Farm with handsome Bear Kurtzman on the cover."

Hal fired his cigar. His expression stayed sober.

"Good try, guy, but even your wisecracks aren't going to lighten the load I'm carrying."

Kurtzman grew deadly serious. "What is it, Hal?"

"I just spoke with Striker."

Kurtzman frowned. "Where was he calling from?"

"It wasn't a call. He was here in person."

"Striker? Here?"

Brognola chuckled. "That's the first time I've seen you flustered, Bear, since... that night."

"Striker was *here*? Is that what you were doing on that walk to... visit April?"

Hal nodded. "The Sarge set it up. He asked about you, Bear. You'll understand why he couldn't stay around."

"Uh-huh, but what the hell, Hal? I don't know much about this hot potato you've dropped in his lap except that it's real hot."

"That's all you want to know, believe me."

"I can live with spy-in-the-dark," the Bear groused, "but what was our man doing here? This is the hottest spot in the world for him."

"No, it isn't. I've just sent him into the hottest spot in the world and, dammit, I can't even tell you where."

"He didn't come by to turn down the mission then?"

Brognola took a long tug on his cigar and filled the air with smoke, watching for a moment as the grayish cloud eddied and was whisked efficiently out through the air ducts above the CRT terminal.

"I wish he *had* turned us down, Bear, and that's the truth."

"Why did he come then?"

"To say goodbye. To us. To April."

"Sounds like he doesn't plan on coming back. Jeez, Hal, is it that tough?"

Brognola rose from the swivel chair and walked toward a wall of computers, his back to Kurtzman as if not wanting the man in the wheelchair to witness what he felt inside, what he could not keep from showing.

"Damn me and damn this world we live in, Bear, but unless Mack Bolan can somehow pull one hell of a miracle together, I've just sent the Executioner to his death."

1

It was a place for death, thought Andrei Mikhalin. The car that he and his partner, Vladimir Gordeyev, sat in was parked well off the road, hidden he hoped, in a cluster of trees.

There was no moon. The darkness amid the trees was inky, impenetrable. A night breeze whined eerily through the branches overhead.

Gordeyev, seated alongside Mikhalin behind the steering wheel of the ancient Moskvitch, broke in on Andrei's thoughts as if telepathically reading them.

"Trees or no trees, we'll be like sitting ducks here if a patrol comes by and they're wearing night vision device goggles."

"It would be better if we did not have to meet the woman first," Mikhalin muttered in an attempt to change the subject. "This is not a woman's place. A woman will jinx us."

"Don't tell me about it," Gordeyev grunted agreement. "It was not my decision."

Mikhalin rechecked the action of the Uzi submachine gun he carried, held low against his lap, his eyes, like his companion's, ceaselessly, nervously, panning the pitch-black night beyond the sedan's windshield. The terrain was tabletop flat for miles in every direction, fertile farmland except for the distant twinkling lights of Moscow's southwestern suburbs.

The two men had been parked at this contact point, 150 meters off a secondary highway, for the past fifteen minutes, it being Gordeyev's custom to always arrive early for connections such as this one.

Especially such as this one.

It was the predawn hours of a weekday morning. There had been no sign of any traffic from either direction.

"It is true the woman is the only one who can positively identify the man we are to meet, this Bolan," Mikhalin groused. "That is but one more reason to worry."

"She should be here," Gordeyev said, nodding. "If the people bringing the American in are on schedule, he or they will be showing up any second now."

"Where can she be?" Mikhalin wondered aloud. "I don't like it."

"So you have told me more than once," Gordeyev snapped peevishly. "I will hear no more of it, Andrei. She will be here. Bolan will be here. We will escort them safely into Moscow, and our job will be done within the hour. Relax. This is not your first assignment for the underground, more like your twentieth, and yet you behave like a novice."

"I know something of this man, Mack Bolan," Mikhalin retorted. "We are in more danger than any of the times before, Vladimir, as is our entire cell, meeting him like this. They call him the Executioner. Did you know that? He is an avowed enemy of the KGB. If we are caught aiding him—''

"His fight is our fight, Andrei. It is true that every other time such as this we have been smuggling people out through this pipeline. Now we smuggle someone in. But we have been asked to help. If we care anything about a free Russia—''

"Yes, yes." The stock of the Uzi felt slippery in Mikhalin's sweaty grasp. "Someday *I* would like to be smuggled out through this pipeline of ours, along with our Jewish friends. Thoughts of Lefortovo or the camps or, worse, the Serbsky Institute—''

Mikhalin broke off, willing himself to think of something else. The current regime was as ruthless and cruel in their treatment of dissidents as any since Stalin, and it could only be worse for he and Vladimir, two known members of an organized underground group.

There was hardly any organization whatsoever in what vestiges there were of an underground resistance movement in the Soviet Union. The group that smuggled Russian Jews to the west, financed by American Jews and the Israelis, had been high on the regime's Active Measures list since its existence had been discovered eighteen months before.

The worst that men such as Mikhalin and Gordeyev feared was the infamous Lefortovo Prison in central Moscow, scene of wholesale torture and execution of dissidents day in and day out. "Special causes," as Andrei knew he and his friend would most certainly be, were far more likely to end up among the horrors of the living dead at the Serbsky Research Institute for Forensic Psychiatry. Dissidents were known to be injected with combinations of drugs that induced schizophrenia, leading to mental and physical deterioration during which one had almost no resistance to brutal KGB interrogation before death.

Mikhalin sensed for the first time the increasing unease of the man who sat beside him.

Gordeyev also held a weapon, a Russian-made Tokarev pistol. He glanced at the luminous hands of his wristwatch.

"The woman is late. You're right."

"I would feel much safer if she had not once been a typist in the army," Mikhalin griped, struggling to keep the tension he felt from showing in his voice. "She could still be working for them—"

"Nonsense. She has proven herself to our cause too many times. She served in Kabul, yes, and what she saw there sickened her. And the way they hounded her family until we got them out . . . no, Katrina is one of us, Andrei. I fear for her safety at their hands."

"And our safety if she's caught and they go to work interrogating her," Mikhalin added. "No one can stand up to the things they do with electricity. Was she not, er, emotionally involved with this man, Bolan, when they met during a mission that took him to Afghanistan? Were they not lovers?"

Andrei was suddenly conscious of something cold pressing against the side of his neck just below his right ear through the open side window. He realized with a skip of his heartbeat that someone had advanced without detection from the darkness to his side of the car, and that the object jabbed against his neck was the muzzle of a weapon.

A woman's voice intoned very low and deadly, "That comes under the classification of private business, my nervous, talkative friend. None of *your* business, am I right?"

Gordeyev started behind the steering wheel, as surprised by the voice as was Mikhalin. He stopped his hand from tracking up the Tokarev when he discerned the vague features of the woman who had so soundlessly crept up on their vehicle.

For his part, Mikhalin stared straight ahead, his forehead beaded with perspiration despite the coolness of the Russian night. He gulped audibly.

"O-of course it is your private business, Citizen Mozzhechkov. I, that is, we, were just—"

The woman eased back on the pistol and holstered it in the belt strapped beneath the jacket she wore.

"You were running at the mouth, citizens, and you would be dead right now had I been a militiaman or KGB. And I do not care for people I barely know discussing my private life."

Mikhalin gulped loudly again. "I am truly sorry, Katrina."

Katrina Mozzhechkov, an attractive dark-haired woman in her mid-twenties, shifted her attention from the men in the car and looked up and down the highway. In the darkness she could see nothing.

"You have been at this work too long, Andrei," she said, not unkindly. "Your nerves are gone. This should be your last assignment for us."

Mikhalin said nothing to that.

"Why did you keep us waiting?" Gordeyev asked. "How long have you been out there?"

She spotted twin pinpricks of headlights rounding a curve half a kilometer to the south, a vehicle of indeterminate size or make from this distance, advancing at a moderate speed toward them.

"It doesn't matter," she snapped in a new tone of voice. "Here they come."

"Or here comes someone," Gordeyev muttered.

"Be ready."

"It has to be them," Mikhalin said. "The patrols would be coming from the city if they were covering this area at all, which they shouldn't be."

"It could be anyone," Gordeyev insisted.

The woman moved away from the car toward wild shrubbery, where she crouched low as the headlights drew nearer, her stomach muscles tensing. She was not sure if it was fear, anxiety or anticipation at seeing a man named Bolan again, and she decided in those fleeting moments, before the vehicle got close enough to identify, that it was most likely a combination of all three.

The memories of her last encounter with Bolan would remain vividly etched in her mind forever.

Bolan was that kind of a man.

It had been less than a year since they had last seen each other, since she had played a part in a Bolan-led lightning commando strike made by Afghanistan's freedom-fighting *mujahedeen* guerrillas against a Russian outpost not far from Kabul.

The Soviet army had been putting the finishing touches on a chemical warfare atrocity dubbed the Devil's Rain, which was intended to annihilate untold thousands of Afghan civilians fleeing through the Khyber Pass to Pakistan.

The fugitives had been trying to escape the scorched-earth policy undertaken by the occupying force as a means of securing a strategically important, backward nation that had the audacity not to willingly bow before the might of the USSR's invasion and takeover.

The Devil's Rain affair had been a violent, bloody campaign for Mack Bolan and for those who had fought alongside him.

During the course of that mission, Bolan and circumstances had fatefully conspired to turn Katrina Mozzhechkov's life upside down. She had been a troubled yet loyal member of the Soviet Union's headquarters office staff attached to the occupying force in Kabul. But once the American had fully opened her eyes to the atrocities being committed every day on the decent people of the rugged land her government had sent her to, she had become a disillusioned soul committed to doing everything she possibly could to aid Bolan's cause.

Bolan's cause for right became Katrina's cause.

It was, she felt, the cause of all who labored and fought for good and decency in a troubled world that seemed to offer no hope except for those who would light a candle in the darkness and fight.

She and Bolan had not been lovers during their short time together. In fact, Katrina had been pregnant with another man's child at the time. She and Bolan had parted ways shortly after the helicopter they had flown from Afghanistan had landed in one of the refugee camps just inside the Pakistan border.

They had not been lovers, no, and yet not a day had passed since then that Katrina did not think of the incredible American. Bolan haunted her dreams, though not in a romantic way.

The father of Katrina's child was dead.

Katrina thought about Bolan because he had changed her life and that of her child for the better; a debt she knew she would never be able to repay. And she thought often of Bolan because she had never met a man like him before or since. She sensed there were very few, if any, men like Mack Bolan.

And now he was coming back into the very heart of Russia to take on odds even greater than she had faced with him in Afghanistan.

Katrina was proud that she had been asked to risk her life to be a part of this, proud to contribute to what the Executioner was coming here to do, whatever that might be.

She watched the oncoming headlights eat up the distance as it moved closer to where she, Mikhalin and Gordeyev waited to guide Bolan to his next contact in the city.

Katrina drew her pistol and waited, the night breeze playing with tangles of her dark hair.

Her heart hammered against her rib cage. Her throat felt dry, constricted. A tremor quivered through her insides, more instinct than rationality, and an instant later she realized what was wrong.

Those lights drawing down on them from the south were not the lights of a car. She could tell now for the first time. The lights were too high off the ground and far apart for any sort of private vehicle, and the engine sound, she realized the moment she heard it, was too deep-sounding and menacing to be a car.

A truck, moving at moderate though steady speed.

Then the concentrated glare of a searchlight stabbed the night in wide swinging arcs perhaps half a kilometer away.

A searchlight mounted on a truck cruising steadily along a secondary country highway at this time of night could mean only one thing, Katrina knew.

It would be a truck full of soldiers on patrol! Army, militia, police, it made no difference.

She had eavesdropped on the conversation between Andrei and Vladimir for some minutes before making her presence known to them, and she quite agreed with Andrei regarding their fate if three dissidents were to be captured together like this.

Lefortovo. The Serbsky Institute. The camps—slave labor for the building of the Siberian pipeline. In any event, imprisonment and death.

She hurried from the shrubbery toward the Moskvitch.

"What shall we do?" Mikhalin whined. "We are trapped!"

"Katrina, could they have been tipped off that we were waiting here?" Gordeyev asked in a calmer voice but with clear concern as the three of them studied the approaching headlights and searchlight that were still two minutes away.

Mikhalin wiped sweat from his forehead with the sleeve of his left arm, raising the Uzi in his right hand. "Perhaps they have already apprehended or killed the man, Bolan, and whoever brought him this far!"

Katrina fought to suppress the anxiety she felt. "A coincidence, this patrol. An act of God," she assured them.

"Hardly that," Gordeyev grumbled.

"If they knew we were here, there would be more of them, plus helicopters with searchlights," she argued, her heart lifting. "If they had captured those we are to meet, they would surely suspect and be looking for us with more force."

The searchlight aboard the approaching vehicle swung in a 180-degree sweep along the vehicle's backtrack to commence probing the gloom along the opposite stretch of road.

"You're right," Gordeyev said, nodding. "We've got a fifty-fifty chance that light won't even touch us."

"We've got to get away from this car in any case," Katrina told them. "If they spot the car, we can take off on foot in three directions before they can call in anyone. The chances are good we can make it safely."

"Nonsense!" Mikhalin snarled. A new strength, the determination of the mortally frightened, did things to his voice. "This is flatland all around here. Turn us around, Vladimir. We can drive across these fields and escape that way, without lights. They won't hear us because of the sounds of their own engine!"

Gordeyev shook his head.

The truck was almost upon them, and from its sound and estimated size Katrina knew it would be a half-ton troop carrier, the kind the army used to routinely patrol the countryside, generally with half a dozen men and a 7.62 mm SGMB submachine gun in a turret mounted behind the cab.

The searchlight continued probing the opposite stretch of highway, the truck's rumbling engine grumbling to less than a quarter kilometer from their position.

"Katrina is right, Andrei," Gordeyev said. "That searchlight may stay on the other side of the road, or it could be in the process of arcing around and miss us altogether as they pass. Or they may turn it off before they reach us. They seem to be randomly looking, no more."

"We shall leave, I tell you!" Mikhalin insisted, real panic claiming him now.

Katrina reached in, touching Mikhalin's shoulder.

"Andrei, you must calm yourself. They are almost upon us," she whispered. "Even if they play the light this way, they may be half asleep at this hour. The beam might escape us or they may not even see us. They would surely observe the searchlight reflected from a moving vehicle and would come after us. Come now, please. You must leave the car with Vladimir and I—"

Mikhalin wrenched his shoulder from her touch, tracking up the Uzi, yielding to his panic.

"If you fools won't drive us out of here, I will!" he snarled, aiming the Uzi at Gordeyev's head. "Get out, do you hear me! I'm taking the wheel. Do it or I'll kill you, Vladimir. I'm not going to die here! Out, I say—"

Gordeyev moved with lightning swiftness, shoving out with his left arm, knocking the Uzi in the direction of the windshield. He started to say something but was drowned out as Mikhalin's trigger finger squeezed off a quick 3-shot burst.

The noise was deafening within the confines of the car, 9 mm slugs disintegrating the Moskvitch's windshield, spraying shards of glass everywhere.

Gordeyev released his own weapon, reaching up to Mikhalin's gun hand in an attempt to wrestle the Uzi from his partner. Mikhalin started to scream something, frightened, panicky.

Katrina leaned into the car and delivered a fast, short chop with her pistol, the gun butt popping sharply against the base of Mikhalin's skull before anything else could happen.

The man sighed, a small bubbly sound, and went limp in the passenger seat. His arms relaxed beside him as he settled back against the car seat like a man who had suddenly fallen asleep.

Gordeyev holstered his pistol. He grabbed the unconscious Mikhalin's Uzi, looking in the same direction in which a tense Katrina already peered with apprehension.

"They heard the shot," Katrina told him.

The Soviet half-ton braked to an abrupt halt for a moment only, the soldier manning the searchlight swinging it around to the side of the road in the direction of the Uzi's reports. The searchlight lanced the gloom, the men aboard the truck obviously holding tight for a moment, trying to locate the origin of the gunfire.

When the spotlight found nothing, the truck, still several hundred meters down the road, resumed moving forward at a slower, steadier pace, the searchlight arcing, probing, concentrating on the Moskvitch's side of the highway now, no more than thirty seconds away, closing in.

Gordeyev glared at the unconscious man beside him.

"Damn you, Andrei, you have gotten us all killed!" He worked open his door, grasping the Uzi in his left hand. He started to climb out of the Moskvitch, right arm wrapping around the chest of the unconscious man, pulling Andrei out of the car with him, saying to Katrina, around Mikhalin's unwieldy bulk, "We can't leave him here. They'll find him. He'll talk."

Katrina nodded. "And he is our friend."

She hurried around the car to assist Gordeyev in trying to get away from there with Andrei before the searchlight picked them out. The truck was now approaching a point on the highway parallel to where the Moskvitch sat in the cluster of trees.

Katrina moved quickly, and with everything else occupying her senses, knowing these next few heartbeats would determine freedom or capture or death, she somehow feared worst of all dying without having seen Mack Bolan once more, not knowing what had happened to him...

She reached the rear of the Moskvitch, angling as fast as she could around to the other side, when the spotlight atop the half-ton's cab swiveled along a fast-moving arc to come upon the Moskvitch and what was happening there.

"Down, Katrina!" Gordeyev shouted in her direction.

The searchlight centered in to cast a brilliant glare around the car.

Katrina dropped to the ground immediately behind the sedan. The car and the earth around it became surreal daylight, everything rendered an unnatural silverish hue that hurt her eyes.

She heard the engine of the troop carrier rev throatily. The driver of the half-ton wheeled the truck off the highway, rolling into high gear as he came toward the car. The man behind the searchlight worked the spot around to keep the target starkly revealed.

Katrina peered around the edge of the sedan's back bumper to see what Gordevey was doing. He had managed to get Mikhalin out of the car, tugging his friend in a sort of fireman's carry. But an expression of mingled fear and effort appeared on Gordeyev's face as he stood, he and his unconscious cargo etched in the brilliant light of the half-ton, which rumbled to within several hundred meters of the Moskvitch.

A shouted command issued from the truck's cab.

"Halt!"

Gordeyev kept on moving from the passenger side of the car, pausing before turning to seek cover with his partner. He twisted around and triggered a blast from his Uzi in the direction of the truck, shouting over his shoulder in Katrina's direction.

"Run, Katrina! Run for your life!"

"Vladimir!" Katrina cried out.

She broke from her hiding spot behind the car to assist in hauling Mikhalin to cover, but even as she started to move heavy submachine gunfire hammered the night apart from atop the half-ton.

Katrina emitted a high-pitched shriek at the sight of an extended fusillade that ripped into the bodies of Mikhalin and Gordeyev. The heavy projectiles shredded the two men, splashing the Moskvitch with blood that glistened wet and black in the starlight.

The gunfire ceased abruptly, its ominous echoes receding like thunder across the farmland and inside Katrina's head as she watched both corpses collapse against the side of the car.

She jerked herself back down below cover of the vehicle.

A weird stillness reclaimed the scene.

A commanding voice from the cab of the half-ton ordered the troopers in the truck to climb out and scour the area.

Katrina fought for self-control, momentarily paralyzed from the shock of having witnessed the violent end of two decent, good and gentle men who had been her friends. She began to shiver uncontrollably.

She willed herself to turn from the Moskvitch, knowing she had practically no chance of escape. She moved stealthily away from the car and got several feet before the searchlight from the truck threw into vivid relief the figures of two soldiers in Russian uniforms, standing directly before her on a small ridge.

Both soldiers stood side by side, their legs spread, aiming AK-47 rifles at her.

"Stay where you are," one of them commanded.

She froze.

The second soldier called to the others beyond the car. "Lieutenant, over here. We found one of them…alive!"

Katrina knew the pistol she held was useless except for one thing.

She started to turn it on herself before either soldier could do anything to stop her.

Two terrible thunderclaps pounded the night in the instant before she could raise the pistol to her head.

She glanced up to see both soldiers pitch face first toward the ground, the back of each man's head rupturing into a fountaining ruination of blood and brains as they tumbled to the rich farm soil.

Katrina started to look around, unable to grasp what had happened.

A strong fist grabbed her wrist out of the darkness and yanked her forcefully to the ground, out of range of the soldiers on the other side of the Moskvitch.

A strong, commanding, unmistakable voice growled in Katrina's ear. "Stay down."

She saw nothing but the night around her here, away from the searchlight.

She sensed shifting shadows as the presence released her, moving away quickly in the direction of the truck.

The other soldiers, in the instant after the two thunderclaps of gunfire, shouted to one another in confusion.

And Katrina Mozzhechkov knew only one thing with any certainty.

She knew what had become of Mack Bolan.

The Executioner had arrived.

2

Bolan sprinted away from where Katrina crouched beneath the ridge of otherwise level terrain. He knew she would be safe there and out of the Soviet half-ton's line of fire.

He angled away from the car, away from the riddled bodies of the Russian dissidents, concentrating on the soldiers by the truck.

Bolan figured the lieutenant would be in the cab next to the driver, already radioing their base camp for support, most likely air cover. He would be jabbering like hell.

The driver inched open his door, easing himself out of the truck cab, an AK-47 assault rifle stuck out ahead of him like the twitching antenna of some insect.

The two soldiers standing in the bed of the half-ton appeared equally nervous in the indirect lighting of the high-intensity searchlight. One of them now manned the light, swiveling it in the direction of his two fallen comrades beyond the automobile, searching for a walking specter he could not see.

The second soldier in the rear of the half-ton stood behind the submachine gun mounted next to the searchlight. The gunner swiveled his heavy-duty weapon in this direction and that, finding nothing to fire at.

The specter that had brought down their comrades evaded the searchlight's glare. Bolan moved like a ghost, soundless, announcing his position while still on the move with another couple of rounds from the stainless-steel AutoMag.

The searchlight burst into almost as many flying bits as the head of the man behind it. The glare of the light was extinguished to the tinkling sound of shattering glass and the toppling sounds of the guy behind it. One of the slugs propelled the soldier backward, and he skidded out of the bed of the half-ton.

Darkness cloaked the scene.

Bolan continued to move, tracking the AutoMag on the spot where he remembered the Soviet lieutenant and his driver were when they had been lined in the spotlight's glow an instant ago. He pegged off two more rounds from Big Thunder.

The driver slammed into his officer inside the cab under the awesome impact of a bullet that cored his heart.

The AK-47 he had been pointing clattered to the ground.

The opposite door of the cab flung outward under the joint force of two dead men, the Russian officer catching the second bullet. Both dead bodies sagged to dangle half in, half out from that side of the cab.

The machine gunner wasted no time in swinging his heavy-duty deathspewer in the direction of the Auto-Mag's flashes. The gunner triggered off a lengthy burst at the spot where Bolan had been but was no more.

The Executioner landed on his belly, coming out of a roll into which he had pitched himself after taking out the two in the cab.

The hail from the submachine gun droned close over Bolan's head.

He aimed from where he lay stretched out on the ground, triggering off a shot from the .44 hawgleg, aiming at a spot just above the pounding submachine gun.

The firing ceased abruptly, and another dead man crashed the gates of hell, the gunner's corpse backflipping over the opposite side of the half-ton.

It took a few more seconds for this gunfire to mumble away into the distance, and by the time it did Bolan had already rushed back to Katrina's side.

The woman, a vaguely discernible figure in the night, leaped to her feet and ran forward to meet Bolan, embracing him with a frantic bear hug. She, in turn, was lifted off her feet for a moment when he returned it.

Bolan stepped back, his left arm around her trim waist, shapely as he remembered it. His AutoMag swept the night, illuminated now only by the headlights of the half-ton.

Utter silence reigned there again except for the squeaking of the branches as they rubbed against one another overhead in a wind that carried the yapping of a distant farm dog.

Bolan knew the peace would not last.

Katrina stepped back, getting an emotional hold on herself, but he could tell she could not stop the tremoring that shook her body.

"Th-thank you . . ." she said weakly to Bolan. "Vladimir . . . Andrei . . . oh, my God—"

Bolan gripped her arm above the elbow. This seemed to stabilize her.

"We can't help them, Katrina. I don't want to leave our dead, but this site will be swarming with helicopters within seconds."

"It . . . is so good to see you, Mack."

"Likewise, but save the amenities," he said with an additional squeeze that seemed to bring her around all the way. He released her. "How much do you know, Katrina? Do you know where you were supposed to take me—the next stop?"

"For you, yes . . . d-don't you know?"

"I'm being fed it piecemeal," he growled. "We've got to get there fast before we pick up a tail. I would guess Niktov."

She nodded, her breathing returned to normal.

Bolan was surprised to see Katrina here. He had thought he would never see her again after Afghanistan, such was the way of his world.

And here she was.

Quite a damn lady, yeah.

Her nod told him his guess about Niktov was right.

"We can drive to meet him in the Moskvitch," Katrina said, turning to the car, avoiding looking at any of the sprawled bodies, friend or foe.

Bolan touched her arm, halting her.

"The lieutenant had time to radio a description of the car."

"Then what—"

"The truck. Let's go."

"But—"

Bolan heard the first faint rotor throbs coming from the direction of the city.

A chopper.

It would be an Mi-24 Hind gunship, responding to the SOS relayed by the Soviet officer in the truck. And there would be more chopper gunships following the Hind.

Bolan grabbed Katrina's hand.

"The truck," he repeated. He took off in that direction, the lady keeping double-time pace with him, grasping his hand for dear life. He guided her to the driver's side of the half-ton. "Can you drive this thing?"

"Of course."

"Take the wheel."

Katrina hoisted herself into the cab. She caught a quick glimpse of the bloody, twisted corpses of the officer and driver leaning out of the opposite side.

Bolan hurried around. He tugged both bodies out of the truck, tossing them aside. He slammed the truck door and slapped it with his fist.

"Take us toward the city!" he shouted to Katrina.

Bolan hoisted himself up into the half-ton's bed, positioning himself behind the mounted submachine gun.

Katrina slipped the idling truck into gear, steering the military vehicle around in as tight a U-turn as possible, upshifting.

The half-ton bumped its way across the open field, away from the car and the cluster of trees and the dead bodies sprawled across the night-shrouded ground.

The truck reached the highway, Katrina turning the rig's wheel sharply and accelerating toward the distant twinkling lights of Moscow's suburbs.

Bolan had other lights to worry about—the flight lights of the approaching helicopter gunship that, now that it was closer, his trained eyes clearly recognized as a Hind.

The noisy gunship closed the distance to overfly the moving truck, banking around to hover about fifty meters overhead.

Bolan heard the dashboard radio crackle inside the half-ton's cab.

The chopper pilot had not yet spotted the fallen bodies in the darkness off the road. Not yet.

Bolan figured he had killed the Soviet lieutenant commanding the slain patrol before he could fully communicate anything more than that assistance was required.

But it had been enough to bring in this chopper with more, no doubt, standing by or already on their way here as backup. Still, the pilot of the Hind had to be confused: the truck calls in for help, help arrives and there's the truck, barreling back toward Moscow, not responding to the pilot and crew of the Hind trying to reach the lieutenant on the tac net.

The hovering copter continued tracking the truck for several more seconds along the highway. The radio inside the cab continued to crackle with increasingly irritable demands from the chopper above.

Bolan knew that the pilot would take some sort of action real soon unless the Executioner seized the initiative. He twisted his body into a low crouch as he swung the mounted submachine gun around and up, tracking on the chopper.

The helicopter was practically on top of them, the throbbing of its rotors enveloping the truck, pounding at Bolan's eardrums, the backwash causing him to blink rapidly.

He saw one of the crew aboard the chopper leaning well out from the aircraft as the pilot maintained his holding position above and just off to the truck's left.

The half-ton obviously showed no indication of slowing or responding to the chopper's demands for a response.

The pilot and crew had to know something was wrong in the twenty seconds or less since the truck had hit the highway and the copter had sailed in to make contact, trying to eyeball the speeding half-ton up close.

Bolan registered one split-second impression of eyes and mouths widening inside the chopper, reacting when they saw his quick swing around of the mounted machine gun. The pilot worked his stick into an evasive maneuver, the big bird wobbling slightly, starting to bank up and away. Too late.

Bolan opened fire with the machine gun, the mighty weapon's reports piercing through the rotoring racket of the copter. The Executioner's entire frame vibrated from the recoil as he rode a very long, concentrated hail of fire.

The warbird took the murderous fusillade from close enough range to riddle the fuel tanks, the rotor mechanism and the men inside, and the gunship disintegrated into an eye-searing fireball that illuminated the night like sunlight.

The explosion was forceful enough to almost flip the speeding half-ton onto its side. The troop truck tilted dangerously without slackening its speed, the pressure of the blast pushing sideways at the half-ton.

Bolan gripped the gun mount, bracing his wide-legged stance against the truck bed, dodging flaming debris from the exploding chopper.

Inside the carrier's cab, Katrina fought the wheel to maintain the vehicle's balance as she upshifted, increasing the truck's speed with all the expertise of a professional driver handling a big runaway rig.

The charred remains of the chopper plummeted to earth alongside the road, receding behind the half-ton that rocketed through the rural countryside. Katrina straightened their course, regaining full control of the vehicle.

Bolan swung his machine gun around on its mount toward the north, toward the city. He saw no signs of any other approaching gunships.

There could be more on the way, certainly, depending on how much of the chopper pilot's demands of the truck had been monitored by the base, which would then be curious about the abrupt end of communication from the chopper. But for now the night sky was clear of everything except stars.

Bolan left the machine gun, negotiated his way over the side of the truck bed and eased himself in through the open side window of the cab.

Katrina was all business, barely glancing sideways as he joined her, focusing her attention on handling the truck, which slammed on through the unpopulated countryside.

"What shall we do now?" she asked him in a steely, controlled tone. "We cannot go far in this truck."

"We'll have to hot-wire the first car we see."

She turned to look at him quizzically. "Hot-wire?"

"Borrow," he translated.

"An automobile is a luxury in Russia," she reminded him. "Not as commonplace as in America."

"The owner will get it back. You're right. We have to ditch these wheels." He glanced ahead toward the outer perimeter of Moscow, the lights of the suburbs drawing closer with every kilometer. Silhouetted in the glow of the skyline, they could discern new neighborhoods of high-rise apartment buildings. "We'll find one within a few klicks."

The woman's eyes scanned the night as she piloted them through the darkness at an excessive speed toward the city.

"We seem to have gotten away," she said.

Bolan nodded, allowing himself to relax a bit. "We seem to," he agreed in Russian. He looked at the lady behind the wheel, studying her for the first time. "It's good to see you again, Katrina," he continued, "although it is quite a surprise."

"It is good to see you, Mack," she replied. "But I wish the circumstances could be...different. Poor Vladimir and Andrei."

"I'm sorry I didn't reach you in time. I was traveling on foot from where my last contact dropped me two klicks up that road."

"I understand," she said. "The cells of our pipeline operate strictly apart from each other, though for a common cause, but our activities are directed by the central group. It is the only way. Informers are everywhere."

"The truck passed me, and I was hoping they'd miss you. They killed your friends before I could reach you."

"Andrei and Vladimir were good men," she said solemnly. "They will be missed. Andrei...what happened, the soldiers being alerted, was his fault, but I do not blame him. I blame those who twisted Andrei. He was a victim of his oppressors as are all Russians these days."

"What of your family?" Bolan asked. "Your parents and sisters. What became of them after your defection in Kabul? And what of the child you carried at the time?"

"My mother and sisters raise her. They live in South America now. I helped them to escape this massive gulag our motherland has become. Shortly after you and I parted ways in Pakistan, I came into contact with Russian expatriates to support and assist what there is of an organized underground in Russia. I offered my services, and they helped me to smuggle my mother and sisters to the west through the same pipeline that brought you in."

"You are a brave woman, Katrina."

"My family had of late been sorely disillusioned by those problems Russia will not face, will not deal with," she said. "My father and mother lost their jobs because of what happened to me, and there was talk of worse happening to them if they did not cooperate in turning me in to the authorities. This more than anything made them want to flee."

"Your father?"

"He and I stayed on here, offering our services to the underground. We smuggle Jews out of Russia and black market goods in. It took us some time to be accepted by the cell we asked to join, but father and I were able to prove ourselves to them.

"My father was killed that first week when a KGB informer reported a truckload of contraband coming in and the truck was stopped," Katrina told Bolan with a sad matter-of-factness. "There was fighting and shooting. My father caught a bullet. His death was swift, for which I am grateful."

"I'm sorry."

"It was the way he would have wanted to die," she said quietly, eyes on the road ahead, "after he saw what our leaders are doing to a great people. He was more alive than I'd ever seen him during the short time we worked together with the underground. I continue to fight in honor of a great man's memory and sacrifice. And because I have nothing else to lose."

Bolan experienced a sudden, profound inner sadness and a sense of deep respect and identification with this courageous soul, with her loss and subsequent commitment to a war that had to be fought, though it could never be won.

Taking on impossible odds was not the point, Bolan knew. For a just cause, regardless of the outcome, the winning was in the fighting.

"You must miss your baby," he said quietly.

"She has a better life," Katrina said, sadness in her voice again. "I do what I do for her also, and those of her generation. The future begins now." She turned to look at Bolan. "You speak Russian better than many of our citizens."

He chuckled without much humor, willing to change the subject if she was. "Thanks for that belongs to the man who taught me. I have friends in the States. They provided me with a new method used by the CIA and NSA to learn languages. It's something I've been working on for a long time."

"Since Strakhov," she said, nodding. "Is he what this is about, your coming into Russia like this?"

"Strakhov is always what it's about," Bolan growled. "Until I get him or he gets me."

Suddenly out of nowhere, a Mi-24 Hind, identical to the one Bolan had brought down several klicks behind them, zoomed low overhead in the direction of the firefight.

At the same time, Katrina nodded in the direction she and Bolan were heading. "We will find a car soon."

Bolan withdrew his attention from the flight of the chopper and saw that the first of the residential and business structures of suburban Moscow were now less than one kilometer ahead, replacing the endless flatlands of farms.

"That chopper will be back after us as soon as he finds what we left for him." Bolan told her. "Step on it, Katrina. We need all the time and luck we can get our hands on."

She nodded, coaxing more speed from the racing half-ton.

The vehicle's headlights probed the darkness ahead of them like two luminous fingers pointing the way.

Yeah.

Deeper into hell.

Into the heart of the enemy.

Into Moscow.

The Executioner had come to shake hell to its very foundations tonight, and the hellfire had already begun, to be followed damn soon by more, much more blood and thunder.

KGB HEADQUARTERS IN MOSCOW is a six-level building with a ten-story addition constructed by German prisoners and slave labor after World War II. The structure overlooks Dzerzhinsky Square, which is named after Felix Dzerzhinsky, first chief of the Russian secret political police after the Bolshevik Revolution.

The center of operations for the Thirteenth Section has the musty, tomblike atmosphere of the rest of the highly guarded complex, which is closely patrolled by a full complement of armed sentries—*raydoviki*, the tough, well-trained army veterans.

Inside, the complex has the look, permeated with tired desperation, seen in most centers of bureaucracy around the world: cramped offices, dingy green corridors lined with frayed red carpet, peopled by apathetic human cogs in a great soulless machine.

The office of Greb Strakhov, head of the Thirteenth Section, was somewhat larger than that of his subordinates, as befitting a man of the Major General's rank, though it was no more well-appointed than any of the other offices in KGB headquarters.

Strakhov retained a military bearing that belied his age, and now he stood brooding at the wide window behind his desk. He sipped tea from his cup, narrowed eyes in his broad, square face seemingly concentrating on the floodlit cupolas and domed grandeur of the Kremlin by night less than half a dozen blocks away.

Strakhov thought about Mack Bolan and how he, Strakhov, would soon have the vengeance he had nursed for so long.

Bolan's death was not far off now.

Strakhov felt it as surely as he knew the sun must rise tomorrow.

Bolan's blood will flow and I shall have my vengeance.

A discreet though brisk knock at his office door brought the KGB commander out of his reverie. He became a bit irritated when he realized that he had somehow lost track of time, so vivid had his thoughts been of a man's imminent death and a score to settle, and how it could well happen before the night ended.

Strakhov returned to the tall chair at his desk and seated himself. He finished sipping his tea, setting the cup down on a saucer next to a second saucer full of lemon wedges.

"Enter."

Major Anton Petrovsky stepped into his commander's office, approached the Major General's desk and handed him a folded, sealed printout.

"This just came in, Comrade General. Code two, for your eyes only."

Strakhov took the message, broke the seal, read its contents and grunted, tossing the sheet of paper aside onto the desk.

"They've lost him. He arrived in Helsinki yesterday afternoon and gave them the slip."

"Then Bolan could be . . . anywhere," Petrovsky said thoughtfully. "If our previous intelligence is correct, we know he will attempt to penetrate Russia."

Strakhov extended stubby fingers to pick up one of the lemon wedges and bring it to his mouth. He sucked on the tart slice as was his custom when some particularly pressing problem vexed him.

"You are new to your appointment, Major, yet you should know something of this fiend who calls himself the Executioner."

"I am cognizant of what my security clearance has allowed me to review, sir."

"Then you know what Bolan wants in Russia. He wants me. He wants *us*." The section head rose from his chair and stepped toward the window again, letting his gaze take in the Moscow night. With hands clasped behind his broad back, he continued to address Petrovsky. "And it is what *I* want, Major. I *want* Mack Bolan in Moscow. It is a mistake he and those who sent him will regret, no matter how prepared they think they are."

"Sir?"

"We know Bolan is penetrating the Soviet Union with no connections on the outside to whom he may turn for help once he is inside Russia, do we not?"

"Yes, sir."

"Then he is walking into a trap from which there will be no escape. I shall see to this personally. I shall see to his death."

The younger officer cleared his throat. "There is, uh, one report you may be interested in, Comrade General."

"Yes, yes, let's hear it. What have you got?"

"A patrol . . . it isn't clear yet . . . on the outskirts . . . a routine patrol, backed up by a helicopter from their base."

Strakhov experienced a strange quickening of his pulse. He turned again to face Petrovsky.

"What happened?"

"There was . . . some sort of fight."

"Fight?"

Petrovsky nodded, appearing uncomfortable before Strakhov's piercing gaze from cold, razorlike slits.

"Yes, Major General. A . . . battle of some sort. Everyone dead, including two bodies identified as known dissidents."

Strakhov sat down, fighting the excitement and anticipation he felt coursing through him.

"Not everyone was killed, Major."

"Sir?"

"The one who killed them, imbecile."

"The . . . one, sir? But there were six soldiers dead on the ground. A helicopter brought down with its entire crew. Could even this Executioner have done so much damage?"

"He has done it more than once, many times," Strakhov grated. "He is in Moscow already. Alert the army, the militia, the police and all of our units, uniformed and plainclothes. I want Moscow sealed so tightly a bird could not escape without notice. Set up roadblocks on all major and secondary arteries out of the city, and double—no, triple—plainclothes personnel assigned to monitor all public transportation."

"With a manhunt of that size," Petrovsky interjected delicately, "we may run into some complications. Coordinating an operation this big on such short notice without actual hard proof that our man is in Moscow—"

Strakhov slammed a clenched fist angrily on his desktop, rattling the saucers and teacup.

"He is not *our* man, Major. He is *my* man. I am going to see Bolan dead within the next twelve hours because it is personal and because he is the Executioner and because of the havoc he has inflicted against Soviet interests. I shall utilize all of the considerable resources at my command and that includes the army, the militia and the police."

"Yes, sir." Petrovsky nodded weakly, contritely, breaking out in a sweat.

"And because I am Major General Greb Strakhov," he finished in the same angry snarl, "they shall do precisely what I desire or heads will roll and careers will be cut short and time will be spent in the prison camps for some and you—you, Major—will be at the head of that list. I *will* get Mack Bolan, and no one will stand in my way. Have I made myself perfectly clear?"

"Yes, sir. Perfectly."

"Then see to it that my orders are carried out. At once."

"Yes, Major General."

Petrovsky rendered a precisioned salute, which his commander acknowledged with a short nod, then the uniformed KGB officer about-faced smartly and exited the office.

Strakhov crossed to the electric hot water pot, pinched a tea bag from alongside it and filled his cup with water that was kept at a constant boil on the custom-designed setup installed to service the section head's addiction for strong black tea.

While he waited for the tea to steep, Strakhov returned to his desk and opened the lower left-hand drawer. He withdrew the holstered Walther PPK kept there but rarely worn or used in the long years since Greb Strakhov had "come in from the cold" to assume his present job behind this desk.

He hefted the automatic, experiencing the barely remembered headiness he always felt when he palmed the small weapon. Strakhov enjoyed the feel, the touch, of the Walther's butt in his palm, like the renewing of an acquaintance with an old friend not seen in a long time yet with all old bonds renewed at the moment of contact.

He reached farther into the desk drawer to withdraw rag, oil and tools and went about dismantling and cleaning the pistol while he thought more about Bolan. He had been obsessed with Bolan for too long, he realized. The first time was when one of the Executioner's missions had sent Bolan to hijack a new Russian helicopter of top secret design.

Bolan had been successful, then, and many times since. But that first time the American had killed the test pilot of the prototype chopper.

That pilot's name had been Kyril Strakhov.

Beloved son of Greb.

The son's mother had died during childbirth when the boy was born.

Strakhov realized that Kyril's death had snuffed out something inside, something that he couldn't name at the time, but now knew to be his final, tenuous link to any semblance of caring or kindness or any other emotion in a cruel, godless world.

Now he was consumed by hate and revenge and the desire to *get* Bolan to settle the blood debt.

In Strakhov's official capacity he also meant to punish the American for all of the damage he had inflicted upon KGB operations around the world. These included both those "officially sanctioned" operations Bolan had meddled in as well as the "private" KGB activities waged by Strakhov's own power block within the far-flung agency.

The Executioner's one-man guerrilla campaigns had taken their toll, yes, but it was mostly because of Kyril that Strakhov knew he could not rest until Bolan was dead.

The eyes of the Thirteenth Section's chief took on a glazed look as he anticipated the Executioner's end, preferably slow and humiliating, as painful as the agony of emptiness Strakhov had carried inside himself since receiving word of his only son's demise.

Bolan, yes.

Strakhov finished cleaning the Walther PPK, then reassembled it. He did not reholster the deadly little pistol at first. He caressed the automatic, gazing down at it in his hand, savoring the feel of it.

The first indications from intercepted U.S. communications had been borne out.

The Executioner had returned to Russia.

To Moscow.

To Strakhov.

Strakhov slipped the pistol into the underarm shoulder holster rig that he had not worn in years, feeling renewed and ready.

Welcome to your execution, Mack Bolan.

He reached for another slice of lemon.

All that remained now, he knew, was the waiting.

Waiting for the kill.

3

Bolan and his female companion appropriated an early model Fiat from the well-lighted parking lot of an eight-story apartment building in the suburbs of the city. They had abandoned the army half-ton on a residential street nearby.

Bolan picked the lock of the Fiat and hot-wired the car while Katrina stood watch nearby. No one saw them, or at least no one tried to stop them, despite the bright illumination of the blacktopped parking area. It was an hour of the morning when everyone in the apartment building and those in the surrounding residences would be sleeping soundly.

Bolan slid in behind the steering wheel and eased the Fiat out of the parking lot, turning on the headlights only when the car was half a block away from the parking lot. He held their speed below the legal limit, carefully obeying all traffic regulations.

Except for the occasional truck hauling fresh produce in from the communal farms to the markets, and several cruising police vehicles that seemed to pay no attention to the Fiat, the area was devoid of traffic at this hour.

Bolan tracked deeper into the sprawling, sleepy metropolis.

Moscow consists of several concentric circles, each new one having been added as the city expanded over the years. The innermost ring is the area around the Kremlin, an architectural hodgepodge of utilitarian office buildings, stately historical sights dating before the Revolution and modern shops and eateries.

The second ring is a garden boulevard, lined with prerevolutionary palaces and apartment buildings. The third ring is another mixture of the old and new and is the major truck route in and out of the city.

The final ring, where Bolan and Katrina had left the truck and acquired the Fiat, is the present perimeter of the city, clogged with new suburbs and high-rise apartment houses.

Bolan's destination was an address in the north end of Moscow in a district near the truck route, the area where much of Moscow's nightlife, and its dark side, can be found.

Moscow, the political, cultural and economic center of Russia, is a depressingly colorless city, lacking even the familiar distractions most westerners, especially Americans, would take for granted, and yet within the confines of its superficial one-dimensionality this large metropolis is a study in contrasts every bit as dramatic as those of the nation itself.

The USSR is the largest unbroken political unit in the world, occupying more than one-seventh of the land surface of the globe.

Bolan knew something of Russian history: an unprecedented epic of endurance, resilience, hardiness and human suffering of almost ungraspable magnitude and scope spanning the centuries.

Half in Europe and half in Asia, Russia's history has been shaped by this basic geographic fact, beginning with the nomads and wandering warriors who inhabited the area as early as the eighth century B.C.

Tradition has it that the Viking Rurik thrust into Russia in 862 A.D. to found the first Russian dynasty in Novgorod.

Ivan the Terrible was the first Muscovite czar in the fifteenth century. Brutally smashing the power of rival princes and landowners with an unheard of cruelty, he also murdered his own son.

World War I brought about the end of czarist rule and the humble beginnings of a future world power. Nicholas II was forced to abdicate on March 15, 1917. He and his family were slaughtered by revolutionists sixteen months later.

The Union of Soviet Socialist Republics was established as a federation in 1922.

At 8.65 million square miles, Russia is every bit the much fabled "enigma wrapped in a mystery" it has always been, possibly more so today than ever before, comprised as it is of 257 million people who are divided into 150 nationalities speaking over sixty-seven different languages.

It is a land varying from the Arctic regions in the north to the subtropics in a small part of the south.

A large country, yes.

A large people of large hearts and souls who lived large, Bolan knew. It is said a Russian may break down in emotional tears over a sad poem one moment and

minutes later become a savage warrior slaying his enemies on the spot.

A brave, basically decent people, no one could ever
doubt the courage of the Russians and their sacrifice in
fighting off the Nazi invaders during World War II, or
in their fierce subsequent fighting to ensure an allied
victory across Europe.

Bolan had no quarrel with the Russian people.

Unfortunately, though, he knew that in far too many
democracies and dictatorships, in history as now, it often
seemed that the wrong ones—those who embodied all of
a society's negativity and none of its promise for a better world—grabbed the power. These were the savages
who had grasped the reins of power even while the Revolution in Russia was in progress, and who repressed a
great people under the heel of domination to this day.

The enemy.

Those to whom power itself was a drug to be used only
to perpetrate oppression and exclusivity, with no intention of sharing it with the people they ruled.

These were the ones resisted by the small, frag-
mented, largely ineffectual dissident underground within
Russia.

These were the ones—the slave masters, the cannibals, the *savages*—whom the majority of Russians sub-
mitted to with only their unending patience and stoicism
to reaffirm their strength and humanity.

These were the ones Bolan had come to kill, bringing
his war to this sprawling prison camp that was mother
Russia.

To this city on the Moskva River.

Except for the occasional directions Katrina gave to the man behind the Fiat's steering wheel, neither of them spoke for a long time.

Bolan felt comfortable with the quiet between them.

Since accepting this mission from Brognola back in the States, his only option was to play this one on the heartbeat, all the way from the start to whatever bloody conclusion resulted.

He always operated with plenty of room to swing, for he knew that in the heat of combat, no matter how well laid out the strategy, there always came that flashpoint when instinct alone marked the cutting edge between death and survival. And at such a moment improvisation, coupled with intuition and capability, became the deciding factors on how Fate's dice rolled, giving one no time for error or second guesses. You lived or you died.

So he did not mind the fact that a careful strategy had not been devised for him to follow, as had happened on more than one occasion when he had officially worked such missions for his government.

Bolan trusted Katrina Mozzhechkov, but that was all.

He had nothing but his own capabilities, instincts and the audacity of the mission itself to see him through.

Katrina broke into his thoughts. "Turn left into this alley," she directed. "We are almost there."

"Will that end your part?" Bolan asked.

He tugged the steering wheel, slacking speed slightly, and nosed the Fiat into the designated alleyway. Illumination from streetlights filtered in at the far end of the alley. This was not a dead end.

Nonetheless, he took his right hand off the wheel, reached cross-body beneath his left shoulder and withdrew the silenced Beretta 93-R.

"I was instructed to accompany you for a while yet," Katrina told him. "Then the truly hard part for me begins. I must... report the deaths of Andrei and Vladimir to our cell leader. I think I may volunteer to tell their widows as well. It only seems right somehow, since I was present when... it happened. I know the wives of both of them, you see. They are my friends."

Bolan doused the Fiat's headlights. The car crawled along, guided by the spill of light at the far end of the alley.

The looming structures on either side of them formed a canyon in this warehouse district.

Bolan's senses were on high alert. He trusted Katrina, yes, but the sleeping city could have been a million miles beyond the walls of the alley, so remote did this scene appear to him, and he was ready for anything.

"Perhaps," Katrina said softly, sensing also the dangers of the gloom enveloping the Fiat, "a mission that begins so badly can only become easier for you, and will end in success."

She held her Uzi up, fanning impenetrable shadows outside the Fiat as it inched along.

"That would be nice, but it never happens that way," Bolan grunted. "It's only going to get worse, Katrina. Where are you taking us?"

"Right here. Stop the car."

He did as she requested, killing the car's engine.

There was no sign or sound of anyone, anything, around them in the night-shrouded alley.

Katrina unlatched her door and got out.

Bolan did likewise, keeping in a crouch close to the car as he came around to join her.

A sudden rattling jerked them both in the direction of the sound, Bolan's Beretta and the woman's Uzi swinging toward it. They held their fire, and an instant later heard the faint, scampering noise of some small animal scuttling away from a dumpster overloaded with smelly garbage next to one of the warehouses.

Katrina moved to the opposite building.

Bolan headed in that direction with her.

The night carried a new, crisp chill, the night wind a biting nip Bolan had not felt in the open country, as if a new weather pattern were easing in.

Katrina located an almost invisible door in the murk of the wall of the building. She pulled the door outward with her left hand, not lowering her Uzi.

The door yawned on soundless, oiled hinges.

She and Bolan had both fallen back to either side of the doorway, their weapons aimed at the even deeper darkness within the gaping opening.

After a moment's pause, during which nothing happened, Katrina stepped forward, vanishing from Bolan's sight.

He stepped in after her, not wanting to follow, preferring to lead, yet understanding that this was her turf, for the moment willing to see where the lady was taking him.

She must have touched a lever or button in the darkness, because without warning a muted, mechanized hum commenced from somewhere below.

Bolan sensed the door to the alley easing shut after them, blotting out even the faint rays of the indirect lighting from the streetlights at either end of the alley, throwing the narrow space around Bolan and the woman into impenetrable murk.

He felt his finger itch around the Beretta's trigger. He did not like this one damn bit.

The whirring sound ceased, and a soft red light filled the space as two doors parted.

The sound had been an elevator coming up to meet them.

Katrina stepped into the elevator.

"We're almost there."

He stepped in to join her.

She slid the compact Uzi by its shoulder strap beneath her short leather jacket, nodding to the Beretta in Bolan's fist.

"And you had better holster that," she suggested with a small smile. "You are in for quite a surprise."

The elevator descended smoothly with the same whirring mechanical sound, then came to a stop.

Bolan decided to follow her suggestion. He holstered the Beretta, though both the 93-R and Big Thunder were only a speed-draw away.

The elevator doors parted.

And Bolan *was* surprised.

The doors opened onto a nightclub scene as raucous as any he had ever seen, stateside or anywhere else.

The subbasement of what had appeared to be a closed-up warehouse in an uninhabited part of the city actually housed a full-fledged American-style bar, packed wall to wall with noisy humanity.

The lighting was dim, and the closely packed tables were filled to capacity. Just as many after-hours Muscovites were crammed along the walls and the bar, which ran from one end of the long, low-ceilinged room to the other.

The soundproofing had to be state of the art, thought Bolan, to contain the cacophony of this crowd.

Somewhere beyond the swirling haze of Russian tobacco smoke a jukebox blared American rock and roll. The bar pulsed to the throbbing music and the constant din of raised voices.

Except for a cursory glance from some patrons and a pair of mean-looking dudes lounging against a nearby wall—heavies who could only be bouncers, Bolan knew—no one seemed to give him and Katrina a second look as they stepped from the elevator into the crowd, the elevator doors closing behind them.

Then the housemen and a few patrons who had noticed Bolan and Katrina went back to whatever they had been doing before these new "customers" had arrived.

Bolan knew he passed muster under the professional eyes of the bouncers only because of the special custom tailoring of his jacket, which had been designed for CIA agents in the field, supplied to Bolan courtesy of Hal Brognola.

The jacket was fashionable enough in a nondescript sort of way and could pass for European or American cut. It was designed to fit the wearer naturally and at the same time disguise the fact that beneath the jacket were one or two pieces of heavy artillery like Bolan's .44 AutoMag and the Beretta with the attached silencer.

He and Katrina eased farther into the crowded barroom.

The patrons around them seemed to have no interest in them at all or in anything else except the hundreds of animated conversations, arguments and seductions babbling all around through the din of music.

Bolan recognized a few of the more notorious denizens of the Moscow underworld, whom he had met during a penetration into the city a few years before, and from his general knowledge of the Moscow underworld updated periodically, courtesy of Bear Kurtzman and Stony Man Farm.

There was Quickfingers, boss of the pickpocket gangs that cruised Moscow's subway system for victims. Bolan also saw Yan the Fixer in animated discussion with three young men, the length of their hair marking them as dodgers of Russia's compulsory military conscription. Bolan knew that at age eighteen Russian males begin two to five years of active service, followed by permanent military reserve.

The occasional hooker stood out, single women gaudily overdressed by Russian standards, isolating prospective customers and closing in amid the rough-and-ready ambience of the coarse, jovial crowd, which paid no mind to the newly arrived man and woman politely elbowing their way toward the bar.

Bolan had taken the lead in front of Katrina in their slow progress through the crowd, but he was still watching her from the corner of his eye, waiting for her to cue the thing in for him.

She glanced around, obviously looking for someone in the smoky haze. The dim glow, provided by neon signs that hung on the walls advertising American and European beers and by soft lighting from behind the bar, did little to help her search.

This was a place where the patrons preferred what anonymity they could find.

The bouncers back at the elevator had also missed the Uzi that Katrina held at her side beneath her jacket. The heavies had kept their attention on the big man in the dark jacket, sweater and slacks.

Bolan sensed that Katrina was coiled tightly, ready to spring.

He started to lean down to speak to her, deciding to find out now what the next step was. He did not feel endangered or even out of place in this obvious den of thieves, but he did not intend to fly blind any longer.

He checked himself from speaking to her when he and Katrina together spotted the young woman standing at the end of the bar between two men.

She was in her mid-twenties, dark tresses framing her face and brushing her shoulders. As Bolan and Katrina approached the woman, he could discern the fine scattering of freckles across the pert nose and high cheekbones. Her complexion was a shade or two darker than the other patrons in the club.

She shared an easy, buddy-buddy camaraderie with the tough-looking men she was talking to, but her brusque manner could not conceal an earthy, sassy sexuality. The bulky dark sweater she wore with jeans also did nothing to hide the shapely curves and full breasts.

Zara.

The Gypsy woman Bolan had encountered in his dealing with Niktov during a previous visit to Moscow.

Bolan had been attracted to the Romany beauty then.

Katrina headed directly toward the trio.

Bolan and Katrina reached Zara and the two men together.

Zara happened to glance sideways just as Bolan and the woman reached her. It was almost comical the way her expression changed when she saw Bolan. For a moment the lovely smile stopped in midchuckle at whatever one of the men was telling her. Her eyes stopped laughing, the smile changing as confusion registered, then Zara's beauty went expressionless.

The two men with her became aware of Bolan and, secondarily, of Katrina.

"You are Zara?" Katrina asked.

Zara turned to meet Bolan's eyes, the hint of mischief playing with the corners of lush, sensuous lips.

"Perhaps you should ask your friend," she said, still looking at Bolan.

Katrina registered some confusion of her own then. "You two know each other? This I was not told."

"I guess the ones who sent you didn't know," Bolan said.

Then, to the Gypsy lovely, "Hello, Zara."

Zara's open right palm blurred around to land a resounding slap across Bolan's left cheek before he could move to block it.

"That is for not saying goodbye," she said furiously in Russian.

Bolan touched his stinging cheek, unable to hold back the smile that creased his face.

"You always were too fast for me, lady."

"And this is because my heart soars to see you again," Zara finished.

She stood on tiptoe, clasping her fingers at the back of his neck, and delivered a smooth, not overly long, kiss, an intimate contact long enough for her fire to touch him, her tongue darting into his mouth, warm lips suctioning with all kinds of primitive need and promise.

Then she released him just as unexpectedly, turned and pounded the bartop.

"Vitali!" she shouted to the bartender, loud enough to cut through the din to halfway down the bar but still ladylike as hell, thought Bolan, "vodka for my friends!" She turned to Katrina, extending a hand, "And who might you be, my dear? Any friend or more of this brute is a sister to me. Or aren't names supposed to mean anything tonight?"

"You...know why we're here?" Katrina asked. "You were described to me." She glanced significantly at the two hulking Russian males who had not moved since she and Bolan had joined the little party. "We are here to see Niktov."

Zara caught Katrina's glance at the two men. "Don't worry about Boris and Igor. They are Niktov's right-hand men. And mine."

"I parked our transportation in the alley above," Bolan said.

Zara turned to Katrina. "You were told to park on the side streets near here like all the others," she reprimanded, nodding to the noisy crowd around them. "We cannot afford to have attention drawn to what we have here. Niktov... has many interests, you know."

"Things went wrong," Katrina began. Her eyes and voice told Bolan she did not know what to make of the Gypsy she had brought him here to meet. She was not sure how to play this. "We thought—"

Bolan took charge. "I need some license plates put on the car," he told Zara. "I thought someone here could help with that."

"You thought right," Zara turned to the two men who flanked her. "Boris, Igor. You heard the man. Plates from the office. You know where. See that they're put on the car in the alley. Immediately."

The two heavies did not look happy about leaving Zara with the strangers, but they also looked as if obeying direct orders from Zara was part of their job. They glowered in Bolan's direction, then eased away from the bar, disappearing into the noisy sea of humanity packing the place.

Bolan had had no doubt Niktov's friends would be able to fix the stolen Fiat with "clean" plates, enabling him to drive it around the city tonight. He intended to abandon the car at the finish of tonight's mission into Moscow. After that the owner would probably get it back. But since the owner of such a machine, living in an upper-class neighborhood such as the one where Bolan had found the wheels, could only be an upwardly mobile member of the Communist party, Bolan felt scant sympathy for him. The new plates furnished by Zara and her friends would prevent the Fiat from being stopped by the first Moscow cop they saw once the car was reported stolen and an APB went out on it.

Bolan had encountered Niktov on a previous mission to Moscow. Niktov's business as a dealer in rare art objects for the Soviet elite had proved an excellent cover for his bread-and-butter business as one of the ranking power brokers in this city's extensive black market.

Black marketeering in the Soviet Union is a thriving industry boasting an annual yield twice that of some small nations. This "underground" trade is supported by the enthusiastic patronage of millions of Russians who, without the private produce stalls, for instance, might well starve, not to mention having to do without blue jeans, music tapes, transistor radios and countless other items the black market gangs deal in.

Niktov, the smoothest art dealer in Moscow, was also the sharpest crime baron in the city, skimming every ruble made in the black market, or someone got hurt.

"Let's get down to business, Zara." Bolan pitched his voice so he and the two women could have their own conversation and not be overheard by the drinking rabble around them. "I'm on a tight schedule. I wish I had time for pleasantries, but I don't."

Zara reached up again and touched the spot on Bolan's cheek where she had slapped him. This time it was a gentle touch. He felt the slightest current of chemistry pass between them at her gesture.

"Perhaps the pleasantries will come...later," she said.

"Zara, I came to meet Niktov. Where is he?"

The Gypsy lowered her soft fingertips from his hard face. She polished off the vodka in her glass. Bolan and

Katrina did not touch the drinks that the bartender had brought.

"Niktov waits nearby," Zara told them. "I will take you to him."

"Why isn't he here?" Bolan's eyes never ceased scanning the crowded after-hours bar. It had not been long, less than an hour, since he had been killing Russian soldiers on the outskirts of the city.

The military and police machines would already be clanking into high gear, he knew, sealing up the city and all possible routes of escape before closing in until they found the man responsible. They could well come looking for him in a place like this, even if Zara and Niktov and Katrina's dissident friends thought it was safe.

It would not do for Bolan to remain anywhere for very long.

"Niktov is having...problems with rival factions," the Gypsy explained. "He does not wish to make himself an easy target."

"That makes two of us. Take us to him."

"Us?" Zara appraised Katrina more closely. "No offense, darling, but I was told your instructions were to deliver my friend here to this place and that would be all for you."

Katrina didn't bat an eye, her face set in grim lines of determination. "My orders were to meet this man and deliver him into the hands of Niktov personally. This is what I shall do. Then my work tonight will be done."

Zara seemed to consider this.

Bolan grunted, "I can find the guy myself, Zara. Don't be difficult."

Her eyes flashed anger, then the Romany woman shrugged. "Very well. I don't see what the harm can be of having one more along. Perhaps I am jealous," she explained to Katrina in a friendlier, easier tone.

"You have no reason to be," Katrina assured her. "I love this man, but not the way you seem to think."

"Ladies, ladies," Bolan chided. He turned to Zara. "Is there another way out of here besides the elevator?"

"There is, but it is best we are not seen leaving."

"What do you suggest?"

Zara's dark eyes twinkled. "Perhaps a slight diversion."

Zara moved so that she was standing between Bolan and the closest male customers lining the bar behind her. She pressed against Bolan, her arms going around him, molding her body to his so he could feel every lush, wild curve straining against him. The perfumed scent of her hair tantalized his nostrils as she moved her lips to his ear.

"Push me," she said fiercely, hotly. "Hard!"

He pushed, shoving her away with enough effort to propel her, into the drinking man at her back. She used the backward movement to jar the man off balance, spilling his drink.

The guy whirled sharply, angrily. "Here, now! What th—"

Zara regained her balance. She spun toward the man, pointing in the direction of two other guys standing nearby engaged in a conversation.

"He did it!" she shouted at the man she had bumped into. "He said he'd kill me if I didn't go with him!"

That was all the guy at the bar needed to hear.

"Did he, now? I'll fix the swine!"

The man reached with one quick movement for a long-necked beer bottle next to him on the bar. He stepped forward, swinging the bottle in an arc that connected, the bottle smashing to bits on the other man's head.

The guy and his friends whirled to glare at the attacker.

The bearlike dude he'd swung the bottle at shook his head to clear it, then barreled forward with a battle cry, head lowered like a battering ram. He plowed into the first man's gut with such force that the two of them flew into a somersault backward over the bar where they commenced trading punches and breaking more bottles over each other's heads.

The first man's buddies dived into the fray with the second man's companions, and soon others joined the melee, pushing and shoving, throwing punches and catching them.

In a matter of seconds a full-scale brawl evolved, women screaming and shouting, trying to get out of the way, lusty curses and laughter floating amid the thudding of fists into jaws.

Bottles and glasses flew everywhere, some connecting against heads, others shattering when they missed and hit a wall or furniture. Chairs and tables flipped through the air, the impromptu slugfest intensifying by the second with all the glee of children on their last day of school before summer vacation.

"This way!" Zara said.

She made a beeline to a place where the bar met the wall, a few feet away from the raging fight. She touched a button below the bartop.

A panel in the wall slid sideways.

Zara entered the secret compartment, motioning for Bolan and Katrina to follow.

"Hurry!" she urged.

Katrina went on through.

Bolan began to follow, but someone tried to take a swing at him. He blocked the punch with his left arm while his right rocketed up with pistonlike force squarely under the other man's chin.

The guy's eyes rolled back in his head, and he went unconscious but remained standing, held in that position by the close-quarter slugging going on all around him.

Bolan unleathered the Beretta, not for anyone in the subterranean brawl, but for whatever he might encounter on their way out.

"We are wasting time, Mack," Zara said impatiently.

He stepped into the passageway.

The panel whispered shut behind them.

Zara had been right. No one appeared to notice their withdrawal; the patrons of the place were having too much fun taking their frustrations out on one another.

Bolan and the two women had stepped into a stairwell. A soft red light, like that in the elevator they had ridden down in, illuminated the narrow ascent to a landing. From there the stairs rose farther, angling out of Bolan's field of vision.

He marveled again at the expert job of soundproofing someone, probably Niktov, had installed in the subterranean after-hours joint. He could not hear the hint of a sound to indicate there was a full-scale battle royal in progress on the other side of the sliding panel.

The women stood against the wall, side by side, waiting for him.

Zara seemed unaware that Katrina had swung her Uzi out from beneath her jacket with a well-practiced flip, all the while eyeing the unknown at the top of the stairs, her shapely legs flexed in a battle crouch, the weapon held in firing position.

Zara started up the stairs.

"I will show you the way."

Bolan moved forward, grabbing her by the arm just above the elbow, checking her progress before she reached the third step.

"I've done enough following tonight," he growled, not unfriendly, to the Gypsy lady. "It's not my style."

He glided past her, taking the lead, easing against the wall, arm bent, the Beretta ready to open up on any danger that might present itself.

Zara trailed two steps behind him, followed by Katrina who covered their backtrack with the Uzi another two steps behind Zara.

Toward the next link in the chain for this meanest hit of all for Executioner Mack Bolan.

Unless something or someone else unexpected got in the way first.

Unless something else went wrong.

It was that kind of a mission, yeah.

All the bloody way.
The Executioner was hitting Moscow.
And the night would only get bloodier.

4

Bolan drove the Fiat through the almost deserted Moscow streets.

Zara sat beside him this time, giving occasional directions.

Katrina sat in the back seat at such an angle that her gaze connected with Bolan's in the rearview mirror as they passed beneath streetlights.

They passed no police cars this time.

The time: 0330 hours.

A street-cleaning machine lumbered ungainly through one intersection to the wide inner circle of the Sadovoye Ring; it was the only traffic they encountered. The sedan crossed one of the bridges over the Moskva River, which appeared far busier than the streets as barges chugged their way up and down the waterway.

They encountered a few vehicles when Bolan steered them along Valivov Street, but the sparse traffic faded to nothing when Zara curtly instructed Bolan to take another turn into a sprawling six-hundred-acre city park—Sokolniki. As they drove along a winding parkway, Katrina's eyes, reflected in the rearview mirror, held wary apprehension, something Bolan also felt.

There had been no conversation among the three of them since leaving the after-hours club. They had reclaimed the Fiat, which Boris and Igor had dutifully supplied with new license plates. The two sad-eyed giants had wanted to come along, but Zara had told them a firm no.

The weather had continued to change during the short time Bolan and Katrina had been in the warehouse. The stars were now blotted out by low cloud cover, and the air carried a brittle chill to it. The night breeze had died down to nothing, and in the stillness Bolan sensed the promise, or threat, of snow.

The coming storm, threatening from the dark sky, matched the rising excitement Bolan felt in his gut. This last link of the chain, he hoped, would send him into the thick of what he had come this far around the world to do.

Get Strakhov.

Then the score for April would be settled.

"There," Katrina said, pointing.

Bolan saw it at the same time. He braked, coasting to a stop on the shoulder of the parkway. He pulled up not far behind a vintage Rolls-Royce that sat beneath the overhanging branches of an ancient tree near a statue honoring the war dead who had fallen fighting the Nazi hordes.

Sokolniki Park was wrapped in a quiet of near total solitude, a far cry from the warehouse district where Bolan had met Zara, but seemingly every bit as remote within the heart of Moscow.

There was a bench situated against the base of a lamppost several meters down along the parkway, the light offering enough illumination for Bolan to clearly make out the three men waiting at the base of the monument.

A hulking bodyguard stood on either side of the bench. They could have been cloned from Zara's friends, Boris and Igor, thought Bolan.

The Executioner approached, glancing about, his senses penetrating the night. They seemed to be alone here—Bolan, the two women, the man on the bench and his two sidekicks—though the lamp glow along the parkway was hardly sufficient to light up much of the ominous gloom.

Bolan strode toward the three men waiting by the monument, leaving his jacket open so he could grab his concealed weapons without hesitation. He did not like the setup here.

"Hello, Niktov."

The elegantly clad, elderly man seated on the bench sat in much the same posture as when Bolan had last seen him. To Bolan it seemed as if time had stood still since their last encounter.

Niktov's clawlike hands rested on a silver-topped cane, his prominent forehead framed with eccentric waves of thinning hair, the black dye job still rather too obvious. The Russian sported a pair of rimless glasses that rode on a beaked nose. As always Bolan was reminded of a schoolteacher.

"Mack Bolan," the "art dealer" acknowledged in return, the inflection of his voice aged but strong and steady. "I have learned your true identity since our last encounter, you see. I forgive you your little charade from the last time, pretending to be of the world of art. Yes, I now know all about you, Mr. Bolan.''

It was made as a simple statement of fact with no apparent malice or implied threat. Bolan centered his attention on the old sharpy. He knew Katrina would be eyeing their surroundings, the index finger of her right hand again curled around the trigger of the Uzi concealed beneath her jacket.

''And yet you agree to meet me here like this,'' Bolan said to Niktov. ''Like spies.''

The art dealer chuckled. ''Yes, indeed. Exactly like spies. And I suppose you would like to know why.''

''I suppose I would, and make it fast. I hear there are people after your head.''

''Some of my, er, business rivals, yes.'' Niktov lost any trace of his good humor. ''You're right. We shall make this brief. Nowhere is safe for me in Moscow.''

''I thought you were the boss.''

''I am, truly, but there is dissension in the ranks, if I may say so. It will only take some straightening out. Negotiations are in progress. And at this moment these rivals I speak of should be under the impression that I am at home in bed, alone and asleep and, might I add, under very efficient personal protection.''

''Then let's hear what you have to say. You know why I'm here.''

Niktov nodded. ''Strakhov.''

''The last time I was in town, you and the Major General were friends.''

''Associates,'' Niktov corrected. ''The Major General is a collector of sorts, as you know.''

''What happened?''

Niktov's face darkened. "I was cheated."

"By Strakhov?"

"None other. To the tune of several hundred thousand rubles...well, more than I could afford, though even that is beside the point. The sordid details need not concern us. Suffice it to say I can abide most anything in my fellow man—" Niktov bowed gallantly in the direction of Zara and Katrina "—and woman, but chicanery...never!"

"This misunderstanding with Strakhov. Does it have anything to do with your black market troubles?"

"Possibly. That would hardly surprise me. Misunderstanding, indeed. The man is a liar and a scoundrel."

Bolan thought of April Rose and of a whole lot of human suffering he had seen since undertaking his unsanctioned activities against the KGB. He thought of atrocities that happened for no other reason than that they helped line the pockets of scum like Greb Strakhov.

"He's a lot worse than that," Bolan told the old man seated on the bench. "What have you got for me?"

Niktov answered with a snap of his fingers. The bodyguard to the art dealer's left stepped across to the Rolls, opened the back door, reached inside and withdrew a slim black attaché case from the car. He brought back the case, handing it to Niktov.

"You perhaps wonder why I risk sitting outside of my comfortable car," Niktov said to Bolan as he took the attaché case from his bodyguard.

"It had crossed my mind."

Bolan felt uneasy. He glanced around them into darkness that could conceal anything.

"I am dying, as are we all," Niktov said. "I am closer to death than most. Months. Weeks. A cancer grows within me. I may be dead before then, if my enemies have their way. They are not content to let nature take its course, it would seem. I rarely go out anymore." He looked skyward. "It will snow. Good. I had feared I would die without seeing snow again."

Bolan nodded at the attaché case. "Is that for me?"

"It is." The Russian extended the case to Bolan. "Here, take it. It is a new life for you, or more likely, I fear, it is your death...."

CAPTAIN ANATOLI ZUYENKO of the Moscow Metropolitan Police lowered the infrared night vision binoculars from his eyes as Sergeant Kulik quietly approached the GAZ patrol car.

"All is in readiness, Captain," Kulik reported in barely a whisper. "Everyone and their equipment is in place."

Zuyenko nodded. "Both entrances to the park have been cordoned off?"

"Precisely as you ordered. BTR-40s at either end of the parkway, and I have positioned seventy men in as tight a perimeter as possible. We await your order to close in."

Zuyenko lifted the binoculars to his face again for another look at the six people rendezvousing two hundred meters away at the base of the war memorial. He did not know what to make of the confrontation between Niktov and his two bodyguards, who had been under surveillance for some time, and the big man and two women who had arrived in the Fiat only moments before. Their arrival, their presence in this Moscow park tonight, troubled Zuyenko because they did not fit in with his plans at all, especially the man.

From his slightly higher vantage point, Zuyenko tried again to get a better view of the imposing new figure who was conversing with Niktov. Zuyenko's force, all heavily armed policemen, had been positioned in a wide circle around the two cars and the people at the monument. The police captain's small army was concealed by foliage, the bends and dips in the terrain and, of course, by the dark shroud of night.

Zuyenko sharpened the focus of the binoculars, but this did little good since the big man speaking with Niktov had shifted his position slightly. His back to Zuyenko now, the new arrival scanned the night around him.

Zuyenko heard himself mutter a curse.

Kulik followed his superior's line of vision.

"It is not the way we had planned it, is it, sir? Could they be emissaries from the other side?"

Zuyenko shook his head. "Niktov is a marked man, Sergeant."

"They must know he has a terminal cancer. Why are you so sure—"

"They must kill him before he dies of natural causes. If Niktov falls and it is their work, if they take out the boss, the others will fall in line."

"Then if the man who has just arrived down there with those two women is not an emissary of Niktov's enemies," Kulik followed through, "who can he be?"

The police captain could see the man in question, his back still to Zuyenko, accepting something from Niktov—an attaché case.

Zuyenko lowered his binoculars thoughtfully. "He appears extremely capable, dangerous, even from this distance. Get on the radio. Inform all units to prepare."

"And the plan?"

Zuyenko glanced at his watch. "We will give the plan...another four minutes. If nothing happens by then, we close in and capture those we have down there now. Do not let any of them leave the park. Especially the big man."

Kulik saluted. "Yes, Captain."

The sergeant turned to the patrol car and the dashboard radio inside.

Zuyenko resumed observing the confrontation taking place below between Niktov and his bodyguards and...*who*?

Anatoli Zuyenko detested uncertainty in all things, especially in an operation like this one. He understood the uncertainties in his plan for tonight, yet the arrival of those three in the Fiat—yes, especially the hulking giant of a man who had driven—presented an uncertainty Zuyenko had not even considered, and so it troubled him, causing his stomach muscles to tense as his throat constricted.

The plan had seemed relatively simple at first.

Zuyenko was in charge of the department's tactical unit assigned to crush the city's black market cartel once and for all, his superiors having grown increasingly adamant in their orders that Niktov be stopped.

And yet the "art dealer" was so clever in his rule over the city's black marketeering, so devious, so well-connected—and Zuyenko knew this meant many who had been bought off—that Zuyenko had become increasingly frustrated with his own inability to arrest Niktov for the crimes everyone knew him to be guilty of.

Zuyenko held no personal hostility toward shrewd old Niktov. Zuyenko's wife shopped regularly for their family's produce at the black market stalls, but that was hardly the point, as Captain Zuyenko's superiors had made increasingly clear.

His career was on the line unless he stopped these black marketeer gangsters, and Zuyenko's bosses were anything but particular about how he did it.

He had worked too hard for what gains he had made in a cold, hostile, impersonal system, and so Zuyenko had gone to work employing decidedly extralegal measures once he had learned of the dissension within Niktov's underworld hierarchy and the fact that a splinter group existed that wanted Niktov dead.

Much careful maneuvering had gone into setting up what Zuyenko hoped would happen in this park tonight. He had had Niktov under constant surveillance, and when the art dealer had slipped away through a secret exit in his apartment house in the Lenin Hills, an escape route Zuyenko had known about—thanks to a paid informer—and so had watched, Zuyenko's men had followed Niktov to this park and had reported to their captain, who had been waiting for this exact situation to occur for ten tense days.

It had looked as if Niktov intended to hole up in his fortresslike apartment for the rest of his short life. Zuyenko had almost begun looking for another idea, but when the call had come less than an hour ago he had known it would work and had gone about setting the rest of his plan in motion: an anonymous phone call to the leader of the rival outfit who wanted Niktov dead and a whispered message saying where the art dealer could be found. Then Zuyenko had deployed his paramilitary tactical unit in a cordon around the monument where Niktov waited.

The plan was a simple one indeed, and considering his concentration of force in the park tonight, the police captain did not see how the plan could fail. He would allow Niktov's underworld enemies to accomplish what he could not. He expected one or more cars full of thugs to come careening into the park any moment now, following his anonymous phone tip about Niktov's whereabouts.

Zuyenko had ordered his units to disperse and seal off the park. They were to do nothing until the shooting near the monument was over, then close in and kill anyone left alive. It would appear as a clear-cut case of underworld vermin killing their own, with the police moving in to mop up.

Zuyenko knew that, with both Niktov and the principal killer squad of his rivals out of the way, Moscow's black market underworld would be thrown into anarchy. He and his men could then move in, pick up the pieces to their own satisfaction and bust the gangs apart once and for all.

He fully expected Niktov's enemies to launch an attack any moment now, though the BTR-40 armored cars hidden behind thick foliage near both entrances of the park had reported nothing since the arrival of the Fiat with the women and the big man in black.

Zuyenko clearly discerned the big man's uneasiness down there. The big fellow spoke with Niktov but never seemed to stop glancing around at the veil of night. He was unable to see Zuyenko's men but, the police captain sensed, the big man seemed somehow aware that all was not right in the park tonight.

A chill ran up Captain Zuyenko's spine.

The big man, whoever he was, looked like a born warrior, a fighter, even with his back turned and at this distance.

He would not be easy to take, thought Zuyenko. The big stranger looked more than dangerous. He looked like walking death.

"INSIDE THAT ATTACHÉ CASE," Niktov said to Bolan, "you will find—"

Katrina stepped forward. "Stop. I do not want to hear this. My work is done. I was to meet this man—" she nodded to Bolan "—and deliver him into your hands," she said to Niktov. Turning to Bolan, she added simply, "I must leave now."

Niktov raised a hand. "My dear, please reconsider. It is late. You will be in danger."

Zara nodded in agreement. "You have come this far with us—" she began.

"It is as far as I wish to go," Katrina said. She turned to Niktov. "I live constantly in danger." She stepped forward, reached up and planted a chaste kiss on Bolan's mouth. "You understand, my mighty warrior."

Bolan nodded. "I understand, Katrina. Good luck."

Katrina said to Zara, "There, you see, now you have no competition for him."

It was not said cattily, merely as a statement of fact.

Zara started to say something, as did Niktov.

Katrina spun on her heel and withdrew at an angle away from the small gathering, heading away from the faint lamplight. She disappeared into the night.

Zara stared off in the direction in which Katrina had gone.

"Foolish one," she sighed.

"Not foolish," Bolan growled. "Professional. She did her part bringing me this far."

"A professional, as you say," Niktov agreed. "The less that woman knows, the less she can be forced to tell if apprehended."

Bolan thought of Katrina's decision to break the news to the widows of Gordeyev and Mikhalin, the dissidents slain on the outskirts of Moscow.

"She's got other work to do," he told Niktov, "and so do we. But first I want to know something. Why you?" He gestured with the attaché case gripped in his left hand, ready to be dropped if he needed to fill the hand with a weapon, fast. "Why are you the one handing me this?"

The art dealer chuckled. "You have lost none of your edge since we last met. I do believe you are the sharpest man I've ever dealt with, Mack Bolan."

"Answer me."

"I am the one with the connections. And I will get even with Strakhov before I die for the misdeed he perpetrated at my expense. Yet even I do not know the *why* of it all, my friend. I was only told—asked, I should say—to play this small part. Now that my part is done, I intend to return home to expire a happy man, knowing I have done what I could to strike down Greb Strakhov. Satisfactory?''

''I'm not sure.''

Niktov ignored the iced response. ''As to the contents of the attaché case,'' the old man continued, ''and what is to happen next—''

IN THE BLACKNESS AHEAD OF HER, Katrina raced, light-footed, toward a break in the foliage. Streetlights from beyond the edge of the park offered the only illumination, and not much at that. The park's healthy turf muted her footsteps as she ran, the shoulder-strapped Uzi held in close against her hip beneath the jacket.

She had paid close attention to the route the Fiat had taken from the warehouse where she and Bolan had connected with Zara. Since the beginning of her association with the dissidents, Katrina did not often venture into Moscow. It was too dangerous for her in the city, but this had been a job she had not allowed to pass by.

It had been so strange, she reflected, meeting Bolan once again, and she recalled her thoughts in the moments before she had met him tonight in that farmer's field outside the city. Romantic thoughts, she realized now, jogging along as fast as she could.

Everything had gone so wrong at that rendezvous in the country. Andrei and Vladimir dead. Then the Gypsy woman, Zara, appearing on the scene. It seemed now that in some ways Katrina had never spent any time with the man known as the Executioner. And she somehow knew she would never see him again.

She gained the break in the foliage and kept on the run. If she had gauged her position correctly, judging from those days in her past when she had lived in Moscow, a metro station should be only a few blocks away.

There was danger traveling on foot, of course, not from any sort of street crime—for all its ills, the System had been most successful in dealing with street crime—but simply because it would be odd for a woman to be traveling alone at this hour.

There was a safe house nearby. If she could reach that, she could move out of the city more freely in a few hours after dawn, provided she was not stopped by a curious policeman. She started thinking of stories she could tell if such a thing happened.

She broke through the space between two rows of manicured hedges and ran straight into the towering form of a Moscow policeman wearing sergeant's stripes.

The man chuckled mirthlessly as she collided with him. He grabbed her by the arm, her gun arm, so she could not swing up the Uzi, and jerked her around.

"And what have we here?" the giant demanded almost merrily.

Katrina whirled under his force, finding herself staring at another man.

A man in plainclothes, but a policeman for all that, she sensed with certainty.

She saw the GAZ patrol car and other dark, shadowy forms, men with rifles, fanning out in either direction on the high ground overlooking the monument where Bolan and Zara stood with the seated Niktov and his bodyguards.

Katrina registered everything at once. She twisted, fighting to tug herself loose from the policeman's grip, knowing she could not break free. She opened her mouth to shout a warning, even if only a scream, so Bolan would know he had been led into a trap.

The plainclothesman by the patrol car saw what she was about to do and stepped forward, snarling at the brute trying to restrain her.

"Kulik, silence her!"

"Yes, Captain."

She heard no more except for the swishing of the sergeant's hamlike fist delivering a punch to the base of her neck before any sound could leave her mouth.

She felt a burst of pain, then everything went black as she lost consciousness, collapsing to the ground.

Zuyenko turned from the scene as his belt transceiver crackled mutedly.

Kulik leaned over the unconscious figure of the woman. He reached down and flicked back her jacket, smacking his lips at the sight of shapely breasts. Then he saw the Uzi strapped beneath the jacket. He tugged the weapon loose and turned with it to Zuyenko.

The captain replaced his transceiver on its belt hook.

"This little one was ready for trouble, Captain. Look."

Zuyenko glowered at the sight of the weapon.

"Forget that. See that she is handcuffed and put in my car. We'll deal with her later. Tell your men to get ready. A car is approaching the park entrance at a high rate of speed." Zuyenko glanced down toward the meet, which appeared to him to be winding down. "And not one moment too soon." He unholstered his Tokarev pistol, trying to suppress the queasy sensation of dread mixed with excitement. "Niktov and the stranger down there with him are as good as dead. The killing is about to begin."

5

"The attaché case contains a latex life mask," Niktov told Bolan, "as well as the forged identification you will need."

Bolan could no longer ignore or accept the itching unease needling his subconscious during the four minutes or so since he, Zara and Katrina had arrived here to meet the crafty old Russian.

The certainty that something was wrong only intensified in the minute since Katrina had taken it into her head to pull a vanishing act.

"I've got to keep moving," Bolan told Niktov. "Who do I look up after I leave here, or is that inside the attaché case, too?"

"Hardly. Your next contact will be the one who gets you inside KGB headquarters and will help you if necessary. If possible, I should say."

Bolan's palm itched to draw the Beretta, so acute had his awareness of danger around them become.

"You're stalling, Niktov." He turned to the Gypsy woman. "Get in the car, Zara."

Niktov chuckled. "Hardly stalling, dear lad. When one is as close to dying as I am, one tends to savor even such prosaic matters as this conversation of ours."

Zara reached the Fiat and started to get in.

"Who, Niktov?" Bolan demanded in an icy voice.

Niktov sighed. "Very well. Forgive my self-indulgence, please. You are quite right, of course. There is no time to lose. The next one you must seek out, after you have donned that life mask, is—"

The shriek of tires screeching across pavement and the throaty roar of a car speeding into a turn toward them interrupted Niktov.

Bolan gave in to instinct, keeping the attaché case in his left fist and hitting a combat crouch as he reached inside his jacket and whipped out Big Thunder. He pulled around to eyeball a ZIL limousine without headlights barreling into sight.

Zara threw herself away from the Fiat, freezing against a thick-trunked tree like a lithe jungle feline poised to respond.

Niktov's two bodyguards reacted to the onrushing ZIL with all the precision of a well-oiled machine.

The Russian hood on the old man's right unlimbered an Uzi submachine gun from beneath his coat while his partner fisted a pistol with his right hand, his left supporting the elderly Niktov who played along in what Bolan recognized as a well-coordinated, preplanned emergency response.

The thug with Niktov guided the art dealer toward the Rolls. His twin scurried in a flanking movement, keeping low, his back to his employer, his weapon held in a two-handed firing stance toward the oncoming ZIL.

The flashy black limo racing down the parkway was almost upon them.

Bolan hurried over to Zara.

The ZIL could be some Party muckety-mucks out joyriding after an all-nighter, nothing more dangerous than that.

Bolan didn't think so. He reached Zara.

The whites of her eyes flashed toward him in the dim light.

"What—" she began.

"Hit the dirt."

He helped her along with a brusque shove.

Zara plowed groundward, her Gypsy anger flaring to form a response that never came.

The American nightfighter held his combat stance.

The ZIL tilted forward into a tire-shrieking halt.

Niktov and his bodyguards reached the Rolls. One of his men tracked a pistol toward the rear door of the ZIL, continuing to block Niktov, while the other hardman reached for the Rolls's rear door handle.

Niktov shouted to Bolan and Zara, "The Rolls is bulletproof! Hurry!"

Bolan maintained his position as the back door of the ZIL popped open.

A guy with a pump shotgun started to climb out.

Bolan fired the instant he saw the shotgun emerge from the ZIL's dark interior, the hand howitzer whamming the night air, almost drowning out the nasty sound of a brain-scrambling slug slapping human flesh. The man uttered a death grunt as he tumbled out onto the blacktop of the parkway, the shotgun falling from his dead grip.

Then the front door of the ZIL popped open and another figure started out.

Bolan tracked the AutoMag in that direction.

The front seat gunner managed to get all the way out of the ZIL, then Big Thunder roared again along with a blistering salvo from both of Niktov's gunmen.

The second ZIL gunner performed a jerky little dance sideways, blood spraying the night. His body slammed into the open front door of the car before collapsing in a lifeless heap.

Bolan started to track the .44 AutoMag back from the falling figure toward a man emerging from the back seat, but the gun crew in the ZIL functioned with the same precision as Niktov's men, hitting with lightning speed, undeterred by the death of two of their own.

The guy who stepped from the back seat of the limo carried some sort of heavy device that he wore like a backpack. It featured a curved tube, which he held in front of him. He stood over the corpse of the first man from the back seat and aimed the contrivance—which Bolan immediately identified as a flamethrower—in the direction of Niktov and his two bodyguards, obviously planning to take out the three clustered together by the Rolls-Royce before swinging the lethal fire-spitting weapon at the single man, Bolan.

One of Niktov's men, or maybe it was the art dealer himself, shrieked in panic at the realization of what had come for them.

The guy by the ZIL triggered the flamethrower.

The weapon emitted a mighty whoosh of sound and fury. A long tongue of fire spat out across the distance to engulf the trio next to the Rolls.

All three men began dashing around madly, human torches wailing in agony. One of them fell and touched off a small fire on the ground, while the other two—it was impossible to identify them anymore—ran in frantic, blind circles during the moments before the licking flames rising from their bodies could claim their lives.

The dude by the ZIL kept his finger on the flamethrower's trigger device, tracking the fire-spewing tube toward Bolan's position across the clearing in front of the monument.

Bolan aimed Big Thunder with both hands and triggered a headbuster.

The head hit tunneled the man's skull, slamming the body backward against the trunk of the limo. The deadly tongue of flame formed a new target as the killer's death reflex action kept the thing going, its redirected line of fire wavering as the man fell, the flames shooting now at the nearby Fiat.

Bolan saw it coming and flung himself on top of Zara to shield her.

The Fiat was engulfed by flame, and the car detonated with a tremendous roar that lifted the small vehicle off the ground, the explosion doubling when the gas tank blew.

Chunks of red-hot flying metal razored in every direction, but at such an angle that none of the fiery shrapnel cut into Bolan or the woman he protected on the ground.

With the power of the blast, the exploding car rose off the ground in an oily fireball.

The stream of fire vanished back into the tube as the dead man behind the flamethrower finally collapsed onto the blacktop of the parkway, his dead finger relaxing from the weapon's trigger.

The ZIL's tires screeched one more time, and the limo jumped forward in a high-speed getaway, front and back doors slamming shut with the momentum.

The muzzle of an automatic weapon nosed out from the lowered back window and opened fire, peppering the area around Bolan and Zara with a burst of projectiles that zinged close overhead and into the branches of the tree, the gunner's aim thrown off by the driver's hasty withdrawal.

Bolan rolled off Zara. "Are you all right?"

The Gypsy woman started to stand. "Y-yes," she muttered, somewhat in shock.

Bolan whirled away from her in the direction of the ZIL rocketing away from them.

The scene in front of the war monument looked as if a war had been fought there.

The bodies of the three slain gunman from the ZIL lay sprawled on the concrete apron at the base of the statue; the smoldering heap of unrecognizable charred meat was all that remained of Niktov and his two men.

The nauseating odor of roasted human flesh hung in the night air, and a grayish haze wafted over the "battlefield."

The ZIL, barreling away without headlights, almost gained a curve in the terrain of the parkway that would take it out of Bolan's sight.

Bolan aimed carefully, his left hand steadying his right wrist, and triggered a round from Big Thunder. He heard the loud bang as one of the limo's rear tires exploded.

The ZIL weaved erratically, the driver fighting frantically to correct the drift of the hurtling limousine, the taillights winking as he pumped the brakes, which only made things worse. Moments earlier the ZIL had accelerated to ease into the curve.

The limo shuddered into a sideways skid, then flipped over, rolling amid the mixed racket of shattering glass, crunching metal and flying hubcaps. A high-pitched human scream emanated from inside the ZIL an instant before the car came out of its third roll to smash lengthwise into a tree.

The sedan burst into flames, torching the tree, too.

Bolan held his shooter's stance and palmed a full clip into the AutoMag's butt while he swung the awesome hand cannon a full 360 degrees, eyes and weapon functioning as one, seeking more targets.

And finding them.

Zara saw it, too.

"The Rolls," Bolan told her.

He gripped the attaché case Niktov had handed him, pulling Zara along with him.

They hurried toward Niktov's Rolls-Royce.

The Moscow park had come alive.

Bolan sensed, *saw*, movement closing in from every direction now in the light of the burning tree. With his own night-honed vision, he verified every quiver of something wrong that he had experienced since arriving in the park less than ten minutes ago.

He and Zara reached the Rolls.

Paramilitary-garbed lines of rifle-bearing policemen swooped down toward the scene by the monument, coming in from the higher ground.

Niktov had been one hell of a hustler while he lasted, thought Bolan, but he was no damn strategist!

Bolan figured the police must have had the whole meet under surveillance, but he did not waste time now trying to make sense of these unfolding events.

The rear corner of the Rolls had been burnt a charcoal black near the spot where Niktov and his goons bought it from the flamethrower, but the luxury vehicle appeared otherwise undamaged as Bolan lunged into the front seat behind the steering wheel.

The Rolls purred to life like a contented kitten oblivious of the carnage befallen this place and that which was yet to come.

Zara leaped into the passenger side, slamming the door even as the big car bulleted away from there.

"Strap yourself in," Bolan instructed.

He steered with one hand while fastening his own seat belt with the other.

Zara's dusky face gleamed with excitement and some fear.

"Niktov said this car was bulletproof!"

"We're about to find out," Bolan growled.

He powered the Rolls into a turn, whizzing past the spot where the ZIL and the tree were burning.

The line of men closing in from all sides opened fire, the rapid reports of their weapons in the open night air sounding like popping firecrackers.

The pinging of dozens of projectiles hitting and bouncing off the Rolls-Royce's armor plating was real enough. The windshield and the closed window on Zara's side spiderwebbed around magically appearing notches carved by the bullets, which did not penetrate but still made it difficult for Bolan to see.

He upshifted and hammered down, knowing damn well that these Moscow cops closing in would hardly leave the road out of the park unattended.

Headlights were coming in fast ahead, and behind, as a look in the rearview mirror told him.

Bolan kept the Rolls's pedal to the floor.

The car picked up more speed.

CAPTAIN ZUYENKO AND SERGEANT KULIK raced down the incline toward the scene of devastation around the war monument.

Zuyenko made certain to stay well behind the advancing line of his men. He noticed Kulik did the same. Zuyenko had no intention of catching a bullet. This night would make his career, not take his life, he told himself.

He and Kulik had left the unconscious woman securely restrained in the patrol car well behind them, and Zuyenko barely thought of her now as he and Kulik reached the monument.

The Rolls sped away, his men firing after it as the luxury machine smoothly took the turn near the burning ZIL.

Zuyenko glanced around at the horror spread out before him.

Three dead men fallen where the ZIL had stood, all three taken out by the big stranger in black.

Zuyenko almost vomited at the sight of what remained of Niktov and his two hirelings.

Sounds of rifle fire peppered the night from the direction the Rolls had taken. At that moment Zuyenko's men should be tightening the circle around it.

Kulik, whom Zuyenko knew had seen combat in Afghanistan before being mustered out and becoming a cop, appeared as stunned as his captain. The sergeant surveyed the wreckage of demolished cars and human remains on the ground around them.

"Whoever that man was," Kulik said in awe, "he certainly knows his business when it comes to killing. Who could he be?"

"We'll find out when he's in the morgue," Zuyenko snapped.

"That Rolls is most likely bulletproof," Kulik offered. "You think he and that woman with him have a chance of escape?"

One of the BTR-40s came slamming in past them, the gunner gripping the mounted submachine gun in the turret for support as the driver gunned the vehicle in hot pursuit of the Rolls. The other BTR-40 would be closing in on the parkway from the opposite direction.

If that would not do the trick, Anatoli Zuyenko had ultimate faith in the ace up his sleeve. He smiled to himself at the thought even as the stench of burning meat pinched and stung his nostrils. He had placed a team armed with an RPG-7V rocket launcher at each entrance of the park, concealed next to the BTR-40s.

"No, Sergeant," he told Kulik, "that Rolls-Royce will not escape. It may be bulletproof, but it is not rocket proof."

Kulik nodded when he remembered. "The rockets will stop them."

"They will indeed," Zuyenko snarled with certainty, "and that big bastard driving the Rolls will be as dead as the rest of them, whoever he is!"

ZARA PEERED OUT through the bullet-webbed wind-shield of the Rolls at the headlights closing in on them on the parkway from both directions.

"There's no escape!" she cried out to the man behind the wheel as the Rolls sped along. "But we cannot give up!"

"I wasn't planning to," Bolan growled.

He did not slack off on the Rolls's speed. He eyed the night beyond the bulletproof glass, rapidly judging his options.

The hurtling luxury vehicle had left most of the Moscow police units behind, the paramilitary cops closing up the flanks of the two advancing lines too late.

Rifles continued crackling from behind, bullets ricocheting off the car.

The ends of both advancing lines continued firing at the Rolls from either side of the parkway, but Bolan's primary concern at that moment centered on the sets of headlights racing to box in the Rolls.

He identified the oncoming vehicles as BTR-40 armored cars.

The turreted submachine guns in both vehicles opened up with steady salvos at the same time, hails of 7.62 mm slugs drumming off the Rolls from both directions, snapping more spiderweb designs across front and back windshields. These bullets did not penetrate either.

Many of the machine gun bursts missed the Rolls altogether and began dropping some of the men closing in from the sides of the road, Moscow cops toppling left and right like bloody bowling pins as projectiles from their own force leveled them along the parkway.

Bolan saw that neither of the BTR-40s showed any indication of slowing down as each armored car shaved the space between them and the Rolls in an effort to stitch the Rolls in a withering cross fire.

Muscovite cops knelt below the errant streams of gunfire from the BTR-40s and continued peppering the receding Rolls with rifle and machine gun fire.

The Rolls was on a collision course with the armored car blazing in from ahead, so Bolan took the only real option he saw open for escape.

He palmed the steering wheel, bracing himself against the seat and seat belt, seeing Zara do the same.

The Rolls bumped off the parkway, jarring mightily as its four wheels bounced across a culvert, speeding directly at the nearest line of men firing at it.

Crouched gunners dispersed in every direction when they saw the Rolls abruptly alter its course and begin heading toward them.

Slugs continued raining in on the speeding juggernaut, inflicting no more damage than before.

Machine gun fire from both BTR-40s ceased as the vehicles commenced braking before colliding head-on, the gunners realizing that some of their fire had felled their own ranks.

The Rolls jounced at full speed along the park's turf.

Bolan saw a flurry of figures dodging frantically to escape the oncoming car, all, except for two, making it.

One man was almost flattened when he failed to scramble out of the path of the Rolls. The left front fender caught him a killing blow that pitched the cop, arms windmilling, like a child's discarded rag doll.

Another unlucky enemy stumbled, screamed and died as the heavy-duty vehicle rode over him, front tires and back pulping the Russian enforcer into the park grass.

Zara gasped in horror.

Bolan whipped the steering wheel to his right again.

The Rolls made a run parallel to the parkway toward the nearest entrance.

He hurriedly scanned their backtrack in the inside and outside rearview mirrors and saw a broken line of Moscow cops stumbling here and there, picking themselves up, stunned by his maneuver of cutting right into them.

Some of the paramilitary force pulled their weapons around, unleashing single shots and bursts that proved ineffectual, while others ran to their fallen comrades.

The BTR-40s bunted each other in their haste to swing around and renew the pursuit.

Bolan saw a plainclothes cop yelling, shouting, waving orders to his men, but it did not appear to be doing much good.

Yeah, thought the man behind the wheel of the Rolls, we just might make it!

He steered the machine back onto the parkway, straightening out the vehicle in a speedup toward the park entrance, which he could now see some two hundred meters along the straightaway. He saw no more headlights coming in from that direction, only city streetlights and the buildings beyond the perimeter of the park. He coaxed more speed out of the Rolls.

The men on foot had been left well behind, the armored patrol cars swinging around fully now to give chase, but Bolan knew they would be no match for the Rolls on an open stretch of street.

He and Zara could outrun their pursuers and ditch the ostentatious wheels before reinforcements could be called in. He only hoped Katrina had made it through the lines of ambushers. He would be able to find out about that through one channel or another as soon as he and Zara broke clear. And if Katrina had fallen into enemy hands, he would not rest until he extricated her.

But first the Rolls had to make the park entrance onto the street.

They almost did.

The Rolls-Royce reached a point one hundred meters from the shadowy entrance archway of the park when an explosion of fire zeroed in at the Rolls from the deepest shadows of the park's perimeter.

Not rifle fire, Bolan's subconscious told him in a fractured instant of realization.

A lengthy trajectory, like a pointing finger of flame, reached out at the Rolls from that direction.

Rocket launcher!

Bolan jerked the steering wheel with everything he had, avoiding a direct hit, but no amount of evasive maneuvering could take the Rolls totally beyond the incoming rocket's deadly path.

The last thing Bolan heard before the explosion was Zara's scream.

Then the rocket hit with a detonating impact that robbed him of all control.

The world was eaten alive by an ear-splitting explosion, the force of the incoming rocket flipping the heavy car end over end, tossing Bolan right along with it.

6

Bolan had no choice but to ride out the tumbling assault of sensation and sound as the Rolls-Royce took the blast of the incoming rocket.

His fastened seat belt held him from bouncing around inside the heavy car, which was little less than a tank thanks to the armor plating installed by Niktov. The only conscious thought Bolan registered during those crazy seconds, which seemed like an eternity, was a degree of surprise that he retained his conscious faculties at all. Something kept telling him he should be dying. Or maybe he was.

The instant the limo stopped its roll, Bolan shook his head rapidly to clear it, automatically reaching to release his seat belt even before his rational mind took stock of the situation.

The ruined Rolls came to rest on its right side, the passenger side.

Bolan steadied himself in the overturned vehicle. In the process he discovered that he had suffered no serious injuries, thanks no doubt to the seat belt. He knew he'd have plenty of aches and bruises once the initial shock wore off, but they would not be enough to keep the Executioner out of action.

Bolan regained his full battle awareness, unholstering Big Thunder. He glanced down at the passenger side where Zara had been sitting. It was flush against the grassy ground. She was still strapped into her seat belt, but it had not saved the Romany beauty's life.

The indirect rocket hit had caught the front end of her side of the car. Either the initial explosion or the flipping of the vehicle had killed her. Zara's head drooped at an impossible angle, neck broken, her dark hair matted against the red meaty mess of her smashed face.

Bolan muttered a hot curse of sorrow and anger, then pulled himself up and out from his side of the car, pushing the driver's door open with his left arm, rapidly hoisting himself out. He dropped to the ground, moving away from the Rolls.

The dark color of his slacks, sweater and jacket blended into the half-light of the parkway. He saw three men advancing warily toward the wrecked vehicle from the direction of the rocket launcher's report. The trio advanced with their rifles held forward in firing position, eyes staring at the wreck from behind their rifles.

Shouts and activity filled the air from deeper in the park. A ragged, formless, full-tilt charge of paramilitary cops was closing in now that the action appeared to be over.

The headlights of the two BTR-40s lanced through the night, racing in his direction.

He saw a GAZ patrol car bringing up the rear from the high ground across from the war memorial. The head honcho, he figured, coming in from the point where the attack had been launched.

From the direction taken by Katrina.

Bolan's senses flared with white-hot rage as he tracked up Big Thunder.

The approaching three should have waited for the main force, but they obviously expected to find nothing but death around the remains of the Rolls, nothing but promotions and decorations in their eyes.

They found death, all right.

Bolan triggered three hammering headeaters from the AutoMag.

Three heads burst into spraying brains and bone chips as the Soviet killers tumbled over one another, their bodies twitching in death spasms as Bolan darted away from the car toward the street directly beyond the park.

He reached a line of tall trees that stood like sentinels along the perimeter. Beyond these the man in black with the drawn AutoMag found a wide sidewalk, deserted at this hour, stretching in either direction along an empty street of characterless office buildings.

The activity within the confines of the park had drawn no curious or frightened observers, the way such a fire-fight might have in a free nation. During business hours this neighborhood would be crowded with employees, but it was a no-man's-land now at 4:15 in the morning, those few souls around only burrowing in deeper from sight or involvement at the sounds of gunfire and explosions.

Bolan hotfooted across the street beyond the line of trees.

The blackness of sky could not be glimpsed above the glow of streetlights, but the brittle cool and claustrophobic feel of snow about to fall had intensified. Threatening clouds hung above the Moscow night. They were as dark as the emptiness Bolan felt inside when he thought of the dead woman he had been forced to leave behind in the Rolls.

He swung up his AutoMag in straight-armed target acquisition as four or five of the enemy broke through the treeline on foot in pursuit across the street. The Executioner pulled off three blasting reports from the stainless-steel mini-cannon in his fist.

Bolan felt uneasy firing on uniformed officers of the law. He had sworn at the start of his one-man "outlaw" operations, in the U.S. and around the world, that he would never fire on law officers, even though he was the most wanted man in the world.

The law was sometimes misguided in Bolan's opinion.

That did not make them enemies.

The police were, in fact, soldiers of the same side, and Bolan had vowed from the outset that he would surrender before he took a cop's life.

This was different. Damn different.

These were the enforcers of the Soviet slave state. These cops were damn well the enemy.

And Zara was dead.

Three Moscow cops across the street caught flesh-shredding projectiles, the headbusters dropping the unlucky ones right into the path of their rushing companions.

Everyone alive scuttled for cover behind the treeline.

Bolan heard the two armored patrol car engines revving, the BTR-40s also unseen for a moment, hurtling toward the park's arched entrance from within.

He dodged sideways, slamming another fresh clip into the AutoMag.

He scurried along the dark face of an office building toward a street corner several hundred paces to his right.

Muzzle flashes winked in the darkness as men commenced firing from under cover across the street.

Bullets chewed randomly at the building where Bolan had fired from, but the nightfighter had already distanced himself well away from that spot, closing in on the street corner.

A compact, a Volvo with headlights off, suddenly sped into view almost at the same instant Bolan first heard its engine sounds through the waves of gunfire and the richochet of bullets behind him.

He froze, swinging the AutoMag on the Volvo.

The car shrieked into a 180-degree turn before the enemy firing from across the street even knew what was going on or had time to pull their fire into this new direction.

The car braked to a stop at the curb a few meters away from Bolan, the driver obviously having spotted him.

He stayed his finger on the trigger, sensing this was not a threat.

More like salvation.

The cops across the street ceased firing.

Bolan spotted a few brave ones sticking their heads out, looking in the Volvo's direction.

The first of the BTR-40s popped its nose through the parkway entrance. The armored patrol car stopped as did the one behind it. In the fleeting seconds it would take the drivers to decide which way to turn into the street in pursuit, a woman's voice from inside the Volvo called to him with muted urgency.

"Get in. Hurry!"

Bolan had no choice.

He darted from the shadowy face of the building, hurrying toward the left-hand side of the car.

"Thanks for the lift." He tugged open the door. "Slide over, please," he requested of the driver before he got a look at her.

The woman sitting behind the steering wheel obeyed.

Bolan clambered in, his nostrils picking up a faint hint of perfume that somehow reminded him of Zara.

He popped the clutch, getting away from the corner down a side street, losing sight of the activity at the park entrance. But not before he caught a glimpse of the first of the armored patrol cars grinding into gear, speeding onto the main thoroughfare in their direction.

Bolan piloted the Volvo down the street past the first intersection they came to. He was running without headlights, too busy planning his next action to take time for a look at the woman beside him.

The Volvo came upon an alley to the right.

Bolan braked, turning.

The car fishtailed crazily but stopped a couple of meters inside the alley without scraping either side against the walls.

It was not a dead end, Bolan was relieved to see.

He kept his foot on the gas pedal, ready to dump the Volvo into gear and bolt if necessary.

A few seconds later the patrol cars raced by on the side street Bolan had just turned off, wailing sirens echoing loudly between the deserted canyons of the sleeping city.

The GAZ patrol car Bolan had spotted earlier in the park brought up the rear, whizzing by after the armored cars.

Bolan still had not paused to glance at the woman who had aided him.

She remained in shadow.

He turned now for a look at her after the police cars flew by the alley without noticing the Volvo.

No other vehicles had joined the chase, at least along this route.

The force in the park would most likely be fanning out on a block-by-block search of the neighborhood. It would not be long before their spreading net came to this alley, but the park was two blocks away.

Bolan had a couple moments to spare. Time enough for a look at this feminine good Samaritan.

It was a night for suprises.

Some good, some bad.

And every damn one of them meaning nothing but trouble, including this one.

Especially this one, thought Bolan when he got a look and identified the breathtaking blonde in a tan trench coat who sat in silence beside him.

"Hello, Tanya," he said.

The hint of a smile, no more, played at the corners of glistening lips, and her eyes danced, glinting at what she must have read in his face.

"Hello, Mack," Tanya Yesilov said. "Welcome to Moscow."

They drove to her apartment on Groholski Street.

Bolan's pursuers had been successfully evaded.

Her apartment was typical of those Bolan had visited during his previous trips to Moscow. An apartment is a luxury even to the upwardly mobile young professionals of the Party, but a skillful hand coupled with an interior decorator's instinct had worked wonders with Tanya's drab, cramped quarters: modern art sketches adorned the walls, the appointments lending the two-room flat a comfortable, lived-in ambience.

The kitchen table is the hub of social life in the Soviet Union. Hosts and guest do not lounge about on living room furniture when they visit or talk business at home, but at a kitchen table, cleared away except for shot glasses and the ever-present bottle of vodka. Bolan did not want a drink and neither did Tanya, her table having been cleared for the attaché case that Bolan had been given by Niktov.

He divided his attention equally between a careful inspection of the case and its contents and of the blonde seated across the table. The Executioner had previously encountered Tanya Yesilov in Iran, of all places, when he had penetrated Teheran to wipe out the corrupt powers who ruled that pitiable hell on earth. This breathtaking blonde had proven to be every bit the enigma at the close of that bloody mission as she had been when she and Bolan had first met under enemy fire. She was an enigma as only a beautiful woman can be, and as a double agent needs to be in the perilous world of espionage.

In fact, Bolan had never learned this blonde's real name. When they had met, she had claimed to be a lower-echelon KGB operative, though he suspected now that the echelon was not so "low" after all, but even that was not real. Tanya—that was the name she went by and the name by which Bolan thought of her—was in reality a double agent: a mole planted by the CIA deep within the Russian government years ago.

He had learned a few things about her during that hard and heavy hit in Iran. Tanya's father was American, her mother Russian. They had met and fallen in love in West Germany. Tanya's mother had died during childbirth, and the father had brought Tanya back to America as an infant.

Years later, when she had been a student at Harvard, the CIA had approached and asked her if she would consider returning to the USSR. They wanted her to pose as a disillusioned young woman, hoping the KGB would recruit her, which they did.

By this time her father had died, and Tanya had told Bolan she had gone along with the ruse, hoping it would satisfy a rootless feeling she had had, a time when something inside told her the world, and things in it that meant something, were passing her by.

Tanya had found meaning in the dangerous world of clandestine operations, though much of her duty, until she had encountered Bolan, that is, had been humdrum routine.

That had changed with a vengeance in Iran.

Bolan had wondered several times, during the months since, what had become of her. He had been able to ascertain through his Stony Man Farm connections that Tanya had told him the truth about her past with the CIA, but everything else, including the lady's real name, was buried beneath need-to-know security.

And now here he sat in Tanya Yesilov's apartment.

And none of the needling uncertainty, the feeling that something was wrong he had first felt in Sokolniki Park, would go away.

And this bothered Bolan because he did not know why.

It was more than what had happened to poor Zara or the uncertainty of Katrina Mozzhechkov's fate. It was a feeling Bolan always got when he undertook these espionage missions.

He viewed himself as a soldier. He did not think of himself as a spy. He had, however, accepted the fact that, in the course of the one-man crusade he had undertaken, he would on occasion need to act as a spy, and a damn good one, in order to reach that point where his soldier capabilities could be brought into action with maximum results.

Bolan had learned, developed and mastered the art of espionage with the same dedication he had applied in mastering the skills of modern warfare. The world of espionage is a jungle as real and fraught with peril as the jungles of southeast Asia. Instinct, ability and luck determine who lives and who dies and when.

Bolan completed his inspection of the attaché case and its contents. He looked up from the laminated, forged identification card, which he placed back inside the case with everything else.

His knowledge of written Russian did not match his mastery of the spoken language, but the Cyrillic script on the card posed no problem for him to translate. He assumed the snapshot in the upper right-hand corner of the card—a gaunt, hard-looking, humorless Russian countenance—would be the way he would look after applying the latex face mask crumpled up in the case, as Niktov had said.

Bolan snapped the clasps of the case shut and asked Tanya, "How did you get to that street corner right on time, and why?"

"You don't sound very appreciative, darling."

"Save the darling. And the evasions."

"Very well, but it is good to see you again, Mack."

They had taken enemy fire together in Iran and now Moscow. Bolan had liked something about her. A lot. She had about her an inbred toughness of spirit and, yeah, she was one hell of a beautiful woman.

"Very well," she sighed. "No evasions. I guess that's second nature in my line of work."

"Give, Tanya."

"I had the park under surveillance. Did Niktov not tell you about me?"

"Niktov is dead."

Her eyes lost some of their toughness, dropping from his gaze.

"I suspected as much when I heard the gunfire. That can only mean they know about us, that it is over before we begin."

"No, it isn't. Niktov seemed to think it was his enemies he had to fear, not ours. That park was crawling with Moscow police, not KGB. If I'm any judge of cops, what happened tonight was a police setup to get Niktov. We got caught in the middle."

"Let us hope you're right." She looked back across the table at him with rekindled spirit. "I am the one Niktov was to send you to after he gave you what is in that attaché case."

"Why couldn't you have gotten me the mask and the ID yourself?"

"It would have been extremely dangerous, even working from the inside. I am not a ranking agent in the KGB, remember. Little more than clerical help, really, and the Company man we are to move into place does not even know what we are up to."

"Does this agent know you work for the CIA?"

"No, and it has been most difficult. You see, he is my lover. His name is Anton. Anton Petrovsky. That is his cover name, I should say. He is a major in the Thirteenth Section, an assistant to Major General Strakhov."

"Now we're getting warm. It's Strakhov I came to Moscow to get."

"It is why I suggested . . . using you," Tanya said, nodding. "It was my idea to bring you here to do this thing. Anton is due here at any minute. You had better slip into that mask. My mission for the Company is to monitor his progress. It was not easy, believe me, convincing several of my superiors in the CIA that the Executioner's services would be invaluable in such a delicate operation as this."

"Let's hear what you and your pals came up with." Bolan nodded to the attaché case, recalling the name on the ID card with the photograph that matched the latex life mask. "Who is Sergei Fedorin?"

"There is no such person until you put on the mask. Niktov's connections were very good. What do you know about the Sixteenth Directorate?"

"About what anyone else knows," Bolan grunted. "Practically nothing. Its existence hasn't even been verified. Its purpose is unknown."

"The Sixteenth Directorate is the KGB's gestapo," Tanya said. "Even your friend, Hal Brognola, has not been advised of this. Even the President of the United States is not cognizant of what the Sixteenth Directorate does."

"If moving Petrovsky into place is the mission objective," growled Bolan, "I don't blame you for sitting on it. Who is Fedorin supposed to be?"

"One of the most powerful men in the KGB," she told him solemnly. "More feared perhaps than even the all-powerful of the Central Committee. Agent Fedorin is one of the Sixteenth Directorate's termination specialists, as they are called, believe it or not. He is part of a self-governing unit, operating freely, its very existence unknown to most within the KGB itself.

"The Sixteenth has full jurisdiction to investigate and deal with any area of KGB operations they deem worthy of their attention. It is rumored they are authorized to terminate even section heads if such action can be defended by the Central Committee. Greb Strakhov is about to be investigated...and terminated. You were briefed on Group *Nord*?"

"I was. Andropov put it together in the mid-seventies. It's made up of the chiefs of all the KGB operational divisions. They meet once a month to coordinate operations."

"Such a meeting is scheduled for this morning at 0800 hours at the Balashika complex," Tanya said. "Strakhov will be there. And so will Agent Sergei Fedorin. I will get you in."

Balashika.

Bolan knew about that complex from his own intel.

It was a top secret KGB site, fifteen kilometers east of Moscow, off Gofkovskoye Shousse, operated under authority of the most sinister division of the First Chief Directorate, Department 8, the KGB unit responsible for sabotage, abduction and assassination, designed to shatter the western alliance and weaken the U.S.

A training school in one area of the Balashika grounds provided instruction in terrorism to students imported directly from Third World countries.

The complex was heavily fortified and defended. Bolan had to agree, after a moment's reflection, that Tanya's plan would get him in.

Not only would he have Strakhov under his sights, but he would also have the perfect opportunity to take out the head of each and every KGB section, which would toss that organization into a tailspin that its present setup might never recover from. After Bolan had made this headshed hit for the CIA, it would be open season on the scum, and any other western intelligence agency could take a bite out of the KGB if it wanted to.

April could rest easy then.

"There's something that needs doing first," he told Tanya.

"Something else? I don't understand. This cannot wait. Major Petrovsky—"

He told her then about Katrina, about the vital role she had played in helping get him into Moscow, and of how he had seen Katrina off just before the Moscow cops had closed in at the park.

"I don't know if they caught her tonight," Bolan finished. "I've got a gut feeling they did. If so, I've got to go in wherever they've got her and get her back."

A pause.

Tanya said with a frown, "This is difficult for me to say, Mack, but in doing so would you not be endangering the mission for which we have brought you here?"

"I brought myself. I owe Katrina too much. If they have her, I'm going to get her back."

"Forgive me for sounding coldblooded," the blonde pressed, "but your Katrina knew what she was getting into. Sacrifice is a way of life in this line of business. The timing of the action at Balashika tomorrow, rather, this morning, is of the utmost importance."

"So is Katrina. You know what they'll do to her, and they won't wait around until I have the time to move. You must have contacts you can call, even at this hour, who can find out if she was apprehended in that park tonight."

Tanya paused again to think about it.

She said in a different, softer voice, "If I were in the trouble Katrina may be in, I would want a friend like you I could depend on, Mack Bolan."

Bolan did not know what to make of Tanya in Moscow any more than he had been able to get a gut fix on the lady in Iran. He thought again of how Niktov had died before the art dealer could tell Bolan the name of his next contact on this hit-and-git strike into enemy territory.

The Executioner had only the word of this beauty, this double agent, that she was to be his next link in the action.

"Make those calls," he instructed her. "Let's find out about Katrina."

7

Greb Strakhov tried to ignore the arthritic aches that told him snow was on the way. The KGB section head pulled the furry collar of his heavy coat tighter around his throat to ward off the chilly wind that stirred tree branches overhead.

He stood on a rise beside the plainclothes police officer, observing the cleanup of the aftermath of what must have been a terrible firefight. This stretch of the roadway through Sokolniki Park looked like a battlefield. The policeman, Captain Anatoli Zuyenko, had called in the mop-up detail several minutes before Strakhov had arrived.

Tow trucks with mounted high-intensity lamps and official vehicles with rooftop flashers cast the scene in stark relief against the night, and to Strakhov the illumination seemed to magnify every detail, every horror, stretched out below them. It was deserted at this hour as he gazed down on the carnage around the marble World War II monument. The corpses strewn along the parkway had already been bodybagged and still lay there.

What remained of a Fiat and, a little farther along, a ZIL limousine that had totalled itself against a tree, which had nearly burned to the ground, had been doused with chemical fire retardant. The wreckage of the cars looked like ghostly growths on the dark ground. Strakhov had seen the overturned Rolls-Royce along the parkway as his own ZIL officer's limo had whisked him into the park. He glanced sideways at Zuyenko.

"A terrible business, Captain, but I do not understand why my presence here was requested."

Strakhov thought again of the Group *Nord* meeting scheduled for three hours hence at the Balashika complex, and of the last-minute details needing his attention at his office in Dzerzhinsky Square prior to that meeting.

"But, of course, Comrade Major General." The policeman tried for a show of contriteness. "I hesitated before calling you, but...well, something does not seem quite right here."

Strakhov scanned downrange across the battlefield, masking his irritation.

"I daresay, but what, precisely, is troubling you, Captain? You are assigned to the black marketeers, are you not?"

"I am."

"And so what has happened here? Some altercation between two gang factions?"

"Exactly, sir."

"And how does that affect the Thirteenth Section?"

Zuyenko shifted his weight uncomfortably. "Er, perhaps not at all, Major General. Perhaps I did act rashly. I, er, that is to say, I'm not so sure now, but I thought you should be advised all the same."

"Out with it, damn you. What have you got?"

Zuyenko briefly sketched for Strakhov the events leading up to the battle that had been fought there. He told him of his plan to set up Niktov along with the art dealer's black market rivals, then close in on what was left after the smoke cleared.

Strakhov felt his interest perk at the mention of Niktov's name but kept this to himself. Few knew of Strakhov's dealings with Niktov. Fewer still knew enough to realize that a Major General in the KGB had nothing to fear from a common policeman such as Zuyenko, even if the plainclothesman had somehow managed to establish a link between the boss of the city's black market and one of the most powerful men in Moscow.

Strakhov's dealings with Niktov had not involved black marketeering in any case, and yet Strakhov concealed his interest only with effort, listening to the police captain describe the flamethrower deaths of Niktov and the art dealer's henchmen. He had had at his disposal the means by which to effortlessly terminate the art dealer, but he had chosen not to, having no way of knowing how much Niktov knew about his, Strakhov's, "extracurricular" KGB activities.

The chief of the Thirteenth Section would have been surprised if Niktov had not kept a file on Strakhov as insurance, to be turned over to the Central Committee in the event of the art dealer's death. Strakhov had intended to get those files for himself, then see to it that Niktov was taken out of the way. The Major General had obtained the files, thanks to a paid informant deep within Niktov's organization, and had been considering the various ways of dealing with the black market boss when reliable word had come that Niktov would soon be dead, anyway, of natural causes.

And now this.

"All went according to plan," Zuyenko concluded. "All dead, as you can see. Niktov, his men, those who came to kill them. All dead, that is, except for two."

"Oh?"

"A man and a woman."

"And who are they?" Strakhov asked. "Where are they?"

"The woman's name is Katrina Mozzhechkov. She broke away from the others when the shooting started. You see, we—"

"Never mind that. Where is she and what have you learned from her?"

"I have had her taken to Lefortovo. My assistant, Sergeant Kulik, took her there immediately in my own car. I have instructed no one to question her until I spoke with you."

"My dear captain, I have long passed my days of interrogating street criminals." Strakhov's curtness dripped acid. The early morning had never been his best time. He decided Zuyenko was an idiot. "You will question the woman. What is she? The mistress of one of these dead? Again, why my presence here? My patience grows short."

"I will try to be more succinct. The Mozzhechkov woman is a dissident. Her father—"

"Yes, yes, I remember the name." Strakhov found himself suddenly more interested, and for a moment could not be sure why, could not pin down something elusive he knew he would remember were this a more civil hour. "Well, that is not all that unusual, is it, Captain? The black market gangs have been working in connection with the dissidents for some time. Their pipelines serve to channel human cargo as well as goods both in and out of Russia, and the two are often mutually supportive. What about this man you mention? Is he the real reason you called?"

"He is."

"Well?"

Strakhov felt a strange, exhilarating tingle course through his body.

Bolan, he thought.

He recalled now that the Mozzhechkov woman had initially defected not too long ago in Afghanistan because of Bolan.

"Major General, the man escaped. He was not one of Niktov's gang nor one of those who killed Niktov and his men. He arrived with the woman and another before the shooting started. The other woman is in that body bag over near the Rolls-Royce. We haven't identified her yet. The man who got away . . . he is difficult to describe, Comrade Major General. I could not get a look at his face even though I had them under surveillance for some time, but there was about this man a . . . a sort of . . . *presence* is the only word I can think of to describe him."

Bolan, Strakhov thought again.

"Proceed."

He barely recognized his own voice.

Bolan is in Moscow . . .

"Niktov handed him an attaché case," Zuyenko went on. "When the shooting began, the man, this stranger, reacted in a way I have never seen a man respond. He is a fighter, Major General. A professional of some kind. Very, very proficient, very deadly. I saw him in action. He killed several of my men. He is either a professional criminal of some sort or someone…in your own line of work, if I may say so. It is to apprise you of this, and for you to see the results of this demon's work, that I called Dzerzhinsky Square requesting your presence.''

Bolan!

Strakhov knew it could be no other.

The militia patrol on the outskirts of the city less than two hours ago and now this.

He realized he was too wrapped up in his own thoughts when he became aware that the idiot policeman was addressing him. Strakhov mentally reprimanded himself. Bolan had this effect on him.

Vengeance is at hand, thought Strakhov, turning back to the policeman. *Bolan thinks he has me. I have him…*

"And so I wondered, Major General," Zuyenko was saying. "Did I do right in sending my man to Lefortovo with the woman? Do you wish to have her detained there for your interrogation?''

"No. I shall leave the preliminary investigation in your capable hands, Captain. I'll have my man, Petrovsky, see to the subsequent questioning. Do not have her moved.''

The policeman's chest swelled with pride at the notion of taking a hand in such high-echelon matters.

"As you wish, Comrade Major General. I leave for Lefortovo at once.''

Strakhov inwardly cursed Petrovsky, whom he had not seen since earlier that morning when Petrovsky had reported on the firefight outside Moscow. He lifted his hand in a gesture of dismissal to the police officer.

"That will be all, Captain. Keep my office advised at once of any other such action as this tonight or tomorrow in or near the city."

"Very good, sir. You know who it was, then, this man I've told you about?"

"I believe I do."

"May I ask, Comrade Major General, what connection this demon could have with black marketeers? Do you think a gang war is about to break out, or—"

"Our friend Niktov had his hand in many pies, Captain. That is all, I think. Now leave me."

Zuyenko fielded this last order with a salute, turned and left Strakhov alone with his thoughts. The major general remained a few minutes more on the low bluff overlooking the site of the Executioner's second strike into his territory in less than two hours. The KGB boss's thoughts touched again on the Group *Nord* briefing, scheduled for 0800 hours at the Balashika complex.

Less than three hours from now.

Strakhov knew why Bolan had come to Moscow on this day, not a day or two before nor a day or two hence but *this* morning. The Executioner intended to be at that meeting, he told himself with certainty.

He turned from the scene of Bolan's latest handiwork and strode back to his waiting car. He would attend to the Mozzhechkov woman in due time, but first, always first, there was Bolan. These next few hours would see a duel to the death between Bolan and him. Strakhov knew there was a real chance that he, Strakhov, would not survive it. But the prospect of dying did not bother Strakhov one little bit if it meant Bolan's death as well.

The chauffeur returned to his place behind the wheel, and the limousine coasted away. The first smattering of faint powdery snow began swirling outside the ZIL's smoked windows as the driver steered out of the park toward the city lights.

Strakhov felt a strange twitch at the corners of his tight mouth. He realized he was smiling.

He had worked long and hard to set in motion what was happening this night.

The end is near.

Thoughts of Bolan's death, of seeing the American's lifeblood spurt red and fatal, brought the tingle back.

There was still much to be done.

And time was running out like a time bomb ticking beneath the city itself.

The devil was running loose in Moscow. The Executioner was spilling blood in the streets with more to follow, but Major General Greb Strakhov could not stop smiling to himself in the darkened tonneau of his limousine.

Everything was going precisely according to plan.

PETER JOHN FARRELL, who had spent so many years as Anton Petrovsky that he sometimes barely remembered his own name, dodged hurriedly down cement steps leading from street level to a tobacconist's shop half a block away from Tanya Yesilov's apartment just in time to avoid the sweep of headlights.

A roving police patrol car cruised into Groholski Street.

Petrovsky, for that is how he thought of himself, even subconsciously, so long had this deception been his, glued himself against the cold brick of the stairwell, fingertips unbuttoning his heavy overcoat, reaching for the shoulder-holstered Tokarev pistol beneath his jacket. He also carried a dagger in the lining of his fur cap.

He watched the headlights flit across the front of the building above him, missing the spot where he hid. The vehicle passed and continued down the deserted street.

He waited until the car sounds died away, then left his concealment, regaining the street where the only light came from lamps at either corner of the block. He hurried along the sidewalk in the direction of Tanya's apartment building.

The snow fell in huge flakes, swirling on the night wind, filtering the distant lamplight into surreal patterns. The fallen snow muted his footfalls.

He rushed across the final distance, his breathing almost deafening to his own ears in the silence. He again reconsidered the advisability of this predawn assignation.

He knew he would be in for a hard time from his superiors at Dzerzhinsky Square, most especially from Major General Strakhov, were it known that he was keeping a rendezvous with a beautiful woman when so much else should be occupying his mind, like the Group *Nord* meeting scheduled at Balashika.

He also had to carry out Strakhov's orders for the city to be sealed off in regard to the "Bolan Problem," as the major general had referred to it a day or so ago. To say nothing of Bolan himself.

Petrovsky figured Strakhov knew what he was talking about when it came to the Executioner. Petrovsky had immersed himself in everything there was to know about Strakhov when he was moved into the Thirteenth Section as Strakhov's assistant.

Major Anton Petrovsky again considered the possible consequences if he were caught visiting Tanya Yesilov at this hour . . . and knew he could not stay away.

He had his key out and ready when he reached the door of the apartment building. He slipped the key into the lock and twisted it. The door opened and he stepped inside with all the ease born of a dozen or more previous visits. He turned to close the frosted glass door behind him.

Another set of headlights blazed into life along the snow-covered street. This vehicle was equipped with a spotlight that lit up the side of the street he was on.

The vehicle began to roll in his direction.

Petrovsky flattened himself as best he could against the row of apartment mailboxes.

The vehicle—he could see now that it was a six-wheeled armored car—crunched over the snow, its spotlight stabbing into the foyer.

The military vehicle cruised past without slowing, proceeding to the next intersection where it turned out of sight.

Strakhov's orders have certainly been carried out, Petrovsky thought wryly. The police, militia and military seemed to be patrolling the city streets heavier than usual despite the weather, which Petrovsky imagined would only hamper things more.

He had received word of the firefight in Sokolniki Park before leaving his office.

It seemed that Mack Bolan had indeed come to Moscow.

The man who thought of himself as Anton Petrovsky continued up the stairs toward his lover's second-floor flat.

He knew he was attractive to the opposite sex, and this natural endowment had served him well during his spying career, in and out of the Soviet Union. Women always fell for Anton Petrovsky, and he was of the philosophical inclination that one should gather one's rosebuds whenever the opportunity presented itself.

And yet he had never known—in any sense—a woman like Tanya, whose ice-blond beauty melted into smoldering fires of unquenchable lust that matched his own when the lights were off and they were between the musk-scented sheets of her bed.

There was no woman like her in Petrovsky's life—even though lately he had sensed an occasional dark moodiness about her—and he knew he would never be able to stay away from her when she called him in the middle of the night with that throaty, seductive voice of hers.

And yet he wondered why he thought *this* summons from her was unusual. She had been so secretive about it. He had read tension in her whispered invitation across the phone line such a short time ago.

He and Tanya both worked at KGB headquarters, not in the same office, but near enough to see each other every day. And he was almost always thinking about her. He knew that wasn't good, but still he couldn't stay away.

Petrovsky knew full well the Company would have another agent, perhaps more than one, planted at various bureaucratic levels in Dzerzhinsky Square. Their jobs: to monitor his reports from a station somewhere in the city.

Petrovsky's situation was far too delicate for him to report directly. The other CIA mole could be anyone—a secretary at the office, perhaps one of his mistresses, perhaps another KGB agent.

Perhaps Tanya, he thought. *Or Strakhov himself.*

He reached the top of the stairs and headed straight for Tanya's door.

He chuckled to himself at the notion of Strakhov himself being a CIA spy. Sure, right. That was how this game made one's mind work.

He wondered, as he knocked lightly on Tanya's door, how Mack Bolan's presence in Moscow would affect Petrovsky's mission for the CIA, or for that matter his job in the Thirteenth Section.

Strakhov had been right during that discussion earlier in the major general's office. Bolan had come after the KGB this time, going for the throat, and Petrovsky was doubly interested in that. The Executioner also happened to be at the top of the CIA's terminate-on-sight listing.

The apartment door drew inward in response to his knock.

Petrovsky wondered where Bolan could be at this moment.

The Executioner could be anywhere.

Then he forgot about everything else, just as he always did, when he saw Tanya.

He noticed, as she opened the door and stepped back, that street clothes hugged her lithe, lovely figure the way he liked to see, but he had expected a nightgown, as usual.

She stepped backward into the room, not flowing into his arms, pressing her figure against him, heating his blood to a boil as was her custom.

He noticed her smile was not the same either—a lover's insight. He stepped into the apartment, starting to close the apartment door behind him.

He wondered what was troubling her.

The icy touch of a pistol barrel kissing his temple from deep shadow behind the door was the last thing he expected, because his attention, every bit of it, had been on the woman he desired. He realized he had walked into a trap when a man's voice intoned from somewhere behind the weapon.

"Hand over your piece slowly, barrel first, and everything will be all right. Maybe," the voice said icily in Russian.

Anton Petrovsky did as he was told, reaching very cautiously for the Tokarev pistol. He tried to read Tanya's eyes.

She turned from him, gliding to the window. She inched the drapery back and gazed down into the street, saying nothing.

Petrovsky also remained silent. He extended his pistol over his shoulder, butt first, as he had been instructed, intuition warning him this was no bluff. He knew the man belonging to that voice would pull the trigger of the pistol at his head and blow his brains all over the apartment.

The gun barrel at his temple did not waver.

Petrovsky did not turn his head, though he did look out of the corner of his eye as the gunman reached with a free hand from the shadow to snare the Tokarev. In that instant he thought he caught an impression of two commanding, steely eyes that matched the mankiller voice.

Petrovsky became aware of one awful certainty as the Tokarev was plucked from his fingers.

He did not know how, but he had found the Executioner.

8

The three of them sat at Tanya's table, she and Petrovsky facing each other, two shot glasses and a bottle of vodka between them forgotten.

Bolan sat at one end of the table, having opted for a cup of strong black Russian tea, the AutoMag and Beretta residing in their holsters beneath his jacket.

The two people with him knew he wore his jacket unbuttoned with reason: both or either pistol would fill Bolan's hands with the first hint of provocation. Petrovsky's Tokarev rested in Bolan's right-hand jacket pocket.

As Bolan had relieved Petrovsky of his pistol, Tanya had told the KGB major, "He is not an enemy, Anton. You must listen to what he has to say and to what I have to tell you."

Bolan had moved to stand in front of Petrovsky, keeping the silenced Beretta aimed at a spot between Petrovsky's eyes. He had had no intention of killing the man who called himself Petrovsky, but the major could not guess that.

The major had remained motionless for long seconds, looking from Tanya to the big man in black aiming a gun at him in his lover's apartment.

"I was not followed, if that's what you were looking out the window to see," he had told the woman when she had turned from the window. "Tanya, what is the meaning of this? You're . . . CIA?"

"I'm not," the blonde had lied, "and neither is he." She had indicated Bolan.

"Do we talk?" The big man's deep voice had seemed to penetrate Petrovsky's very soul. "Or do you die?"

Petrovsky had studied Bolan long and hard then, just as he did now, a few minutes later, as he, Tanya and Bolan sat around the table.

But the man that Petrovsky was staring at was *not* Bolan, thanks to the latex life mask. Niktov had provided a state-of-the-art model of the type of mask that has become more and more commonplace in the illusionary hide-and-seek world of spy versus spy.

Tanya had assisted Bolan in applying it in front of the medicine cabinet mirror in her bathroom before Petrovsky had arrived. Applying a life mask was another of the espionage skills developed by Bolan during his Stony Man Farm days, when the full array of equipment of the American intelligence community had been at his disposal.

A life mask is attached to the wearer's face by spirit gum. The porous mask molds itself to the wearer's features, allowing the natural eyes, mouth and nostrils to operate unhindered while the mask alters the shape of cheekbones and forehead. Theatrical makeup is used to disguise where the "fake face" ends and the real flesh of the wearer's neck begins.

A phony mustache completed the facial features seen by Anton Petrovsky or anyone else looking at Bolan.

Bolan disliked the mustache. It irritated his nose but was necessary to conceal the tiny lines that connected the mask's narrow strip between nostrils and mouth. In the right light they would be noticeable to a sharp eye.

"It appears I have no choice but to listen," Petrovsky said now at the table. "We will talk. For a moment...I thought you were someone else. May I ask who you are?"

"I am Sergei Fedorin," Bolan told him, "of the Sixteenth Directorate."

"The Sixteenth Directorate?" Petrovsky repeated with a surprised blink. "But I thought—"

"It does not matter what you think," "Fedorin" interrupted harshly.

Bolan reached into an inside jacket pocket.

Petrovsky jerked back, eyes widening, then he relaxed when he saw the big man produce a slim leather ID packet.

Bolan flipped open the bogus identification for Petrovsky.

"I hope you will forgive me, Anton," Tanya said, "but I had no choice. Comrade Fedorin showed up an hour ago and instructed me to phone you and tell you to come over. I'm sorry."

Petrovsky—that is how Bolan thought of the guy, not knowing the Russian's real name—reached across the table. He patted Tanya's hand reassuringly. "I understand."

Bolan saw clearly how infatuated Petrovsky was with Tanya. The Executioner wondered briefly how much each of them really felt for the other. If these two CIA agents had actually fallen in love, would it affect his mission? He could say nothing regarding this, though. It would be obvious to anyone with half an eye that Tanya and Petrovsky felt a fondness for each other, no matter how real or feigned, but "Sergei Fedorin" would hardly be expected to give a damn, which is how Bolan played it.

He snapped shut the phony ID, repocketing it.

"You will cooperate, Major?"

"As I say, it appears I have no choice. I have heard rumors of the Sixteenth Directorate, of course, but…can you refer me to anyone who could verify who you are?"

"You don't seem to understand," Bolan snarled. "You have two choices: cooperate or die, now that you know who I am. If you cooperate and repeat any of what is said between us to anyone, I will kill you. The same applies to the woman, as I've told her. People do not find out that there is a Sixteenth Directorate until it is too late. The two of you are lucky. I demand your assistance, not your lives. Unless you choose to be troublesome."

"May I ask what you want with Tanya? She is but a secretary. What possible use—"

"It is because of her lowly position that her assistance will not be suspect," Bolan snapped.

"And what of me?" Petrovsky asked.

"You will find that out at Balashika."

"Balashika? The Group *Nord* briefing?"

"I will be at Balashika," the Executioner told him. "There will be death at that meeting. You will live."

Petrovsky got it then.

"Strakhov?"

The "Man from the Sixteenth Directorate" nodded, not breaking eye contact with the KGB officer.

"Strakhov, and others."

Petrovsky rapped his knuckles lightly on the table-top.

"I knew it. I knew there would be trouble. I haven't been assigned to the major general long but...Comrade Fedorin, I don't mind telling you in light of who you are and what you say that I have been . . . noticing things."

"What sort of things?"

"Small incidents that would mean nothing, taken individually, but in light of what you say . . ."

"Yes?"

"Well, I have been instructed to leave the major general's office on several occasions when he was making or receiving what I'm sure were official calls. I am supposed to be privy to all goings-on at the office. And then there was the flare gun."

"Tell me about that."

"I happened into the office early one morning to catch up on some paperwork. Strakhov was receiving the thing from another man in the outside office when I walked in. They reacted in a rather surprised fashion. The major general rarely, if ever, displays any sign of emotion, but it was an unguarded moment.

"I picked up the distinct impression that it was something he and the other man did not want me to see. They quickly wrapped it up in oilcloth and stepped into Strakhov's private office. The man left a few minutes later without the oilcloth."

"Did you recognize him?"

"I've seen him around. He's KGB, from one of the other sections. I can find out if it's important."

"Probably just a carrier from the supply section. Do you know what Strakhov did with the flare gun?"

"I'm sorry. I do not."

"It's the why of it all that concerns me," Bolan wondered aloud. "What you saw supports what we of the Sixteenth Directorate already know to be true."

"And what is that, may I ask?"

"You may not," Bolan snarled. "I think I'm through with you here, Major. You may leave us. And don't miss that Group *Nord* meeting or it's your life as sure as you're sitting here."

Petrovsky chuckled humorlessly. "I'm afraid it would be a race between you and the major general to see who had my head if I missed that briefing."

Tanya cleared her throat right on cue. "May I hazard a guess, Comrade Fedorin? There has been word of Major General Strakhov's, er, extracurricular activities using KGB cover—"

Bolan barked back at her, also right on cue. "Your job was to arrange this meeting, Citizen Yesilov. I'd advise you to let it drop there if you value your life." Bolan glared at Petrovsky. "That will be all, Major." He slid Petrovsky's pistol back to him across the table. "Go."

Bolan did not miss the long look Petrovsky sent in Tanya's direction.

Tanya kept her eyes averted.

Petrovsky did not like it, but the curt order from this man from the Sixteenth Directorate brooked no questioning or denial. He holstered his pistol beneath his jacket.

"Very well," he said.

The major stood and exited the apartment without looking back, leaving the full shot glass of vodka untouched where he had been sitting. He closed the door after himself.

Bolan eyed Tanya as the blonde watched Petrovsky leave. He could not decipher the emotion he saw flicker in her eyes. He waited until they were alone before he spoke.

"Do you think he bought it?"

She thought about that for a moment, then nodded. "I think so. Like myself, Major Petrovsky, whatever his real name, has spent enough time immersed in the KGB to know those we work with are capable of anything. Life, dignity, mean nothing to them. Yes, Anton believed what we told him. Ironic, is it not? Three of us, Americans in a common cause in a foreign land, sitting at this table, talking to each other, pretending to be what we're not. What a strange world this is."

"And what do you pretend to be that you're not, Tanya? Whose side are you on really?"

She flashed him a smile. "Confusing, isn't it? Would you believe the truth if you heard it?"

"Probably not," he admitted, disarming the barb with a chuckle. "I hope we're on the same side."

She lost her lightness of eye and voice. "I know something of your work, Mack. You are new to this espionage game, but it is happening to you as it happens to all of us. No one knows whom to trust. Most of us do not even trust ourselves." The eyes and voice softened again. "In any event, I don't believe you have any choice

WOULD YOU BELIEVE THESE MEN CAN HOLD YOU CAPTIVE IN YOUR OWN HOME?

MAIL THIS STICKER TODAY

WE'LL SEND YOU
4 FREE BOOKS

JUST TO PROVE IT.

See inside for details.

Discover Gold Eagle's power to keep you spellbound . . .

WITHOUT CHARGE OR OBLIGATION

Good books are hard to find. And hard men are good to find. We've got both.

Gold Eagle books are so good, so hard, so exciting that we guarantee they'll keep you riveted to your chair until their fiery conclusion.

That's because you don't just read a Gold Eagle novel . . . you *live* it.

Your blood will race as you join *Mack Bolan* and his high-powered combat squads—*Able Team, Phoenix Force* and *SOBs*—in their relentless crusade against worldwide terror. You'll feel the pressure build page after page until the nonstop action explodes in a high-voltage climax of vengeance and retribution against mankind's most treacherous criminals. *And* you'll also receive our newest high-powered entry Vietnam Ground Zero—fiction drawn from fact that brings the 10,000 day war home as never before!

Get 4 electrifying novels—FREE

To prove Gold Eagle delivers the most pulse-pounding, pressure-packed action reading ever published, we'll send you

4 novels—**ABSOLUTELY FREE.**

If you like them, we'll send you 6 brand-new books every other month to preview. Always before they're available in stores. Always at a hefty saving off the retail price. Always with the right to cancel and owe nothing.

As a Gold Eagle subscriber, you'll also receive . . .
- our free newsletter, AUTOMAG, with each shipment
- special books to preview free and buy at a deep discount

Get a digital watch—FREE

Return the attached Card today, and we'll also send you a digital quartz calendar watch FREE. It comes complete with a long-life battery and a one-year warranty (excluding battery). *Like the 4 free books, it's yours to keep even if you never buy another Gold Eagle book.*

RUSH YOUR ORDER TO US TODAY

YOU CAN'T PUT
A GOOD BOOK DOWN

Razor-edged stories ripped from today's
headlines. Page-crackling tension. Spine-
chilling adventure. Adrenaline-pumping
excitement. Do-or-die heroes. Gold Eagle
books slam home raw action the way you
want it—hard, fast and real.

but to trust me as things now stand . . . with time running out.''

"You're right," he growled. "I've been here long enough. I need you to find out if they're holding Katrina Mozzhechkov and if so, where.''

She frowned. "You will not reconsider? This mission of yours to strike at Balashika, to destroy Strakhov, to move Petrovsky into place, is so terribly important.''

"We've been through this, Tanya. Do you help me or not? I can find her without you. It would just take a little longer.''

She smiled at that. "I believe you could. I believe you would. Very well.''

As he watched and listened, Tanya made a call from the wall phone near the table. She tried two numbers and received no answer, but the third call got it. Bolan had no idea whom she spoke to on the other end, but her side of the conversation was curt, monosyllabic, except for her inquiry about Katrina's fate. She mentioned no names.

Bolan had the impression that whoever she pumped for information was not too excited about giving it out. She replaced the receiver and turned to face Bolan.

"They have her.''

His heart sank. "Where?''

"Lefortovo.''

He finished off the strong black tea in his cup, feeling the mildly rejuvenative effect of the caffeine on his system.

"Then that's my next stop.''

"Lefortovo? But . . . along with the Kremlin, Lefortovo Prison is the most heavily guarded area in Moscow!'' she told him. "It is a prison, after all. It would be suicide for you.''

"Where are they holding her in the prison? Did you learn that?''

"On the third floor of Building D, third door from the end.'' She watched him intently. "It is the largest building at the southwest corner of the prison. My information is that they are to begin interrogating her any moment. Perhaps they already have. The order comes directly from Major General Strakhov himself.''

Bolan buttoned his jacket and started toward the door, toting Niktov's attaché case with him.

"I've got to move fast. They won't spare any means of torture if Strakhov links her to me.''

"A police captain named Zuyenko is in charge of the interrogation,'' she said. "He is the one responsible for what happened in the park tonight. An attempt to trap Niktov and his enemies, as you thought. I know of this Zuyenko. He is said to be a sadist. A truly evil man, as is the one who serves him, a Sergeant Kulik.''

She stood to join him at the door, where Bolan paused for a moment with a hand on the doorknob.

"As a spy for the CIA, I cannot condone your endangering of the mission like this, but as a woman . . . I can only hope you reach your friend Katrina in time. Good luck, Mack. I'm afraid you're going to need it. You'll also need a car.''

"I'll get one. It won't be the first one I've stolen tonight.''

She turned to her purse nearby, unclasped it and returned, extending car keys to him.

"Take mine.''

"I don't want to lead trouble to your door."

"If anything happens," she said uneasily, "I will tell them my car was stolen. Please. My soul would not know peace if I knew I didn't do what I could to help you and Katrina."

He took the keys from her. "Thanks, Tanya. I'll be back in time, or I won't be back at all."

"I would like to see you again, mister," the beautiful blonde told him fervently. "And . . . you *can* trust me."

She moved in against him then, her arms snaking around his neck. She lifted her face to his and delivered a brief, fiery kiss of tender promise. Then she stepped away and watched him ease out of the apartment.

Bolan retraced his way down the back stairway that he and Tanya had come up a short time earlier after parking her car in the designated stall adjacent to the rear of the apartment house. He moved down the steps two at a time, staying close to the wall so as not to squeak any loose steps.

He expected anything.

He encountered no one.

He made his way out the back door of the building and eased toward the Volvo, thinking about the angles and complications of what had hardly been a simple job to begin with but had only grown more labyrinthine with each new twist, each new death. It was a mission that seemed to have fallen apart except for Bolan's determination to do what was right.

The death of Niktov, the deaths of the dissidents, Andrei and Vladimir, would have been reason enough to abort a mission of such importance as this, but there were three reasons Bolan would not, could not, allow himself to even contemplate slowing down on this kill hunt.

Katrina.

Bolan would never allow that good, decent, fighting soul to languish in enemy hands. He had marveled at the difference in Katrina since the two of them had taken fire together in Afghanistan.

The lady who had been a tormented soul at war with herself then had evolved into the confident warrior Bolan had met tonight. In some ways it seemed as if he had just met her.

Bolan's military specialty, dating back to Nam, was striking at heavily fortified enemy strongholds.

No, he would not leave Katrina in enemy hands. No way.

He would bust that lady out if he had to shake Lefortovo Prison down stone by stone, and the fury building in his gut almost made Bolan think that, yeah, maybe he could do just that.

He would get her out if it cost him his life.

And, yes, this soldier knew it could come to that.

Unbidden, mental images of other casualties in his seemingly endless war, dating back to the deaths of his own mother and father, spurred Bolan on.

The Executioner would give anything he had to bust Katrina Mozzhechkov out of that snake pit.

He spent thirty seconds on a thorough search under the Volvo's hood. With a flashlight he had found in the glove compartment, he checked the whole car, but he found no bombs, no homing devices.

He got in, cranked up the engine and backed out into the falling snow, angling toward the street.

The snow would slow him down.

Strakhov.

Reason Number Two Bolan would not let this one go.

He would have the KGB boss in his sights within hours if the mission got that far, if he made it through the hit on the prison.

For a chance at Strakhov, Bolan knew he would travel to the ends of the earth. He had, in fact.

And the third reason that fed the fire in Bolan's gut.

The memory of April Rose.

This one's for you, April.

Hell, yeah.

He headed toward central Moscow, toward Lefortovo. The Swedish car handled well on the snow. He saw more activity in the streets now than there had been only a short while earlier, but it was still dark.

Bolan glanced at his watch.

0500 hours.

The human machinery of the Soviet bureaucracy was clanking awake, early risers already walking or driving here and there through the snow on the way to their jobs.

Bolan was thankful for their presence as he steered the Volvo into the flow of traffic of a secondary thoroughfare, their presence making the Volvo inconspicuous as he drove along.

He thought about Tanya. He did not know what to make of that breathtaking blonde. He was a soldier, not a psychoanalyst.

Tanya.

A beauty, yes.

He could not deny what clicked between them, as it had in Iran not so very long ago. He had often wondered what had happened to her, and now he knew, but still he wondered.

And Zara.

Another fallen ally in this War Everlasting that was Bolan's life.

A man did not turn from his duty, to Bolan's way of thinking, and his duty was to even the score for all the Zaras and Aprils and maybe, just maybe, manage to put a few new wrinkles into the scheme of things somewhere along the way. Perhaps someday the good ones could look out for themselves.

This Executioner wanted more than anything a world where his type of man was not needed, but he did not think there was much chance of seeing such a world in his lifetime.

A lifetime that could end tonight.

And the bottom line.

The mission.

Helping a spy named Tanya ease another spy named Petrovsky into place.

And, yes indeed, time was running out.

For Mother Russia and for an Executioner named Bolan.

The assault on the Balashika complex, the Group *Nord* meeting, would take out the brains behind the KGB's world network of terror.

Or it could be the last mission Bolan ever undertook.

The latex life mask that had turned him into Sergei Fedorin was good for only a maximum of twelve hours and could begin loosening on his face within ten.

He coaxed as much speed as he could from the Volvo as he steered toward his destination through streets made treacherous from the snow.

It was *hard* time, yeah.

Kill time.

The stage was set.

And only Fate knew what would happen next.

9

Hal Brognola could not curb his impatience.

The head honcho of Stony Man Farm was no stranger to the Oval Office of the White House. His liaison activities between the President and the Farm were of such a nature that presidential briefings had become the norm for a Fed cop who, less than a half dozen years before, had been chasing Mafia hoods up and down the mean streets.

He still longed for those days on occasion. Life had seemed so much simpler then, though he understood this was far from the case.

It was never a "simple" job when it came to hunter and hunted.

In most ways, he realized anew, nothing had really changed at all, at least not as far as his work and Mack Bolan were concerned.

The ante had been upped, damn straight, but the one constant between then and now was that Brognola was still the guy who tried to keep it together on the home front while a good man, the best buddy a guy could have, put his life on the line for a government that had put the Executioner atop its Public Enemy list.

To Brognola's way of thinking, Bolan was the best buddy America had in these troubled times.

Make that…mankind's best buddy, Brognola tacked on mentally.

Yeah, it had come to that.

Two husky Secret Service agents, clad almost identically in nondescript conservative suits, accompanied him along the carpeted hallway toward the President's office. A third White House staffer intercepted them with a metal detector device with which he fanned Hal from top to bottom. The man clicked off the device.

"One moment, please, Mr. Brognola. The President is expecting you."

The White House agents at Hal's side faded back.

The "doorman" turned to knock discreetly on the oak door and stick his head in when a voice responded from inside. He twisted the knob, pushed the door in and stepped aside, holding it open as he turned to Hal.

"Please step right in, sir."

Brognola nodded and walked past the agent, who closed the door behind Hal, leaving him alone with the President and one other.

Heavy drapes drawn against the daylight lent a more tomblike ambience than usual to the Man's inner sanctum.

The atmosphere crackled with tension.

The President and the other man stood from a loose circle of wing chairs near the big desk. The President stepped forward, extending a hand, his countenance serious, yet cordial as ever.

"Hal, good to see you."

They exchanged a handshake.

"Sorry it couldn't be under more pleasant circumstances, sir."

"There are no pleasant circumstances in our work unfortunately," the Chief said. He indicated the man with him. "Hal, this is William Brooks. You two gentlemen have met, I believe."

The other man nodded, not offering his hand. "We have."

"Let us be seated then and get down to the business at hand."

Hal joined them, sitting in one of the chairs. He had met the recently appointed head of the CIA twice before and had not liked him either time. The guy's presence here now gave Brognola a sinking feeling in his gut.

"We've received verification on the subject's penetration into the Soviet Union," Brognola began.

Brooks nodded. "Our Helsinki section got us word as well. I don't suppose Stony Man Farm has a monitoring station inside the USSR?"

Brognola bristled at the guy's tone. "I don't suppose we do."

The President, sensing the sparks between two key men, cleared his throat.

"The CIA has received word, Hal, that all hell is breaking loose over there."

"That was the idea, wasn't it, sir, when it was decided to send Striker in?"

"It was," the Man agreed uneasily. "Only it now appears that the action has spilled over into the private sector."

"How's that, sir?"

"A man named—" he glanced at the CIA boss "—Niktov, wasn't it?"

The Company head nodded, glaring at Brognola.

"We've used Niktov several times in the past year alone," Brooks told Brognola. "He was a valuable source of intelligence, heading the black market as he does, uh, did."

"We know about Niktov," Brognola replied. "And you should know that he's had one foot in the grave for the past year. Cancer. What happened to him?"

"We're not exactly sure at this point," Brooks replied. "We have most of the Moscow agencies—police and militia—wired, but nowhere near as well as we'd like to. We'll get more. It's 5:30 in the morning Moscow time so the intel is coming in bit by bit."

Brognola's rein over his patience weakened. "What's coming in, dammit?" he demanded of the CIA chief. "Are you telling me our man took out Niktov?"

"It appears so. Niktov was the second-to-last link Bolan was to connect with after he penetrated Moscow."

"Bolan and Niktov have had dealings before, haven't they?" the President inquired.

"Yes, sir," Hal said, nodding. "And all I can say is, if Striker *did* liquidate Niktov, which I'm not sure he did yet, none of us are, but *if* he did, he can only have had a good reason."

"I wonder," the CIA boss growled skeptically.

Brognola bristled at that, too. "Look, our two agencies have never seen eye to eye. Stony Man Farm is a quick-punch, hard-strike military operation. The Company is hush-hush spies, and agency rivalry is the name of the game in this town. But don't forget, friend, it was your agency that came up with this brainstorm to send Bolan in there to do your dirty work, your killing, for you."

"We didn't want Niktov hit," Brooks countered. "I don't mind telling you it took some long, hard convincing on the part of my staff before I consented to this idea. Dammit, I don't go along at all with the unsanctioned goings-on Bolan has been carrying out, and don't think for a moment we aren't aware that your operation is supplying him with all the assistance he needs."

"Prove it," Brognola growled.

"Gentlemen, gentlemen," the President murmured.

"You're damn lucky," Brognola snarled at the CIA man, "that Bolan didn't tell me to spit in your face when I hit him with this crazy scheme of yours. He had every right."

"We, er, may be willing to offer some unofficial hands-off amnesty to Bolan when this mission is concluded, Hal," the President assured Brognola, "but I'm sure you can appreciate the CIA's position on this, too. They've worked hard to get their man, the one who calls himself Petrovsky, into place. I must say I share their concern."

The Company chief nodded agreement. "The chance of moving Petrovsky up another notch and taking out the heads of Group *Nord* are the only reasons I consented to bringing Bolan in. He's certainly proven himself more than capable at pulling off such actions in the past, and he is our only chance. But personally I think that mad dog killer belongs more on a wanted poster than he does representing this country with his outlaw activities.''

Brognola checked himself from taking a swing at the guy.

"Name one of your operations Bolan has ever screwed up," he demanded testily. "Name one of your agents whose death he was responsible for. Or would you prefer I cited the instances, like this one, where the guy pulled your agency out of the fire? Or the number of your agents who owe their lives to the Executioner?"

The President spoke up. "I think," he said to Hal, "the apprehension is that Bolan will do more to damage Petrovsky's situation than help if his activities take him outside the KGB sphere, as in the case with this Niktov."

"But we don't *know*, sir, if Striker is responsible for terminating Niktov. He's no mad dog killer. You, of all people, should know that."

"It is true I've seen him in action," the President agreed. "I'll never forget the sight of Bolan terminating a KGB spy in this office. I know what you're saying, Hal, and yet you must understand the Company's point of view."

"I'm not sure I do, sir."

"It's simple," the CIA boss grumbled. "We stand to gain if he takes out Strakhov and Group *Nord*, and if Petrovsky moves up a couple notches. On the other hand, we stand to lose a damn sight more if the whole thing falls apart and Bolan fails. And if he starts to take out the wrong people, like Niktov, well . . . maybe he has gone kill-crazy after all, if he wasn't before."

"Like hell he has," Brognola argued. "I guess it's up to you, sir," he said to the President. "Are you going to send the best man we have into the middle of hell to do the impossible for you, then cut off his lifeline and let him die inside Russia with no way out?"

The President of the United States sighed with all the weight of his job apparent in every line of his familiar features, making him appear older, sadder, than he ever had in campaign pictures.

"God forgive me, Hal, but I just don't know. I will hold off making a decision, for another hour or two at least, until we get more information from Moscow. Yes, Bolan is the best man we have, but…if it comes to that, we may have to sacrifice him."

Brognola could not believe his ears, but he held his tongue. The President stood, the meeting obviously over, giving Hal Brognola a whole new gutful of worry.

He had no way of contacting Striker inside the Soviet Union. Brognola's job had been to pass along the government's offer to Bolan; the rest had been orchestrated by others.

Bolan had agreed to go along with it when he heard about the chance to get Strakhov, and the opportunity to advance an agent buried in the KGB's hierarchy.

Had he set Bolan up for the biggest double cross of all?

Bolan had agreed to go along with this mission because he trusted Brognola, and for no other reason.

Were Bolan's instincts right all along?

Was it possible for a man of Bolan's intensely personal moral vision and sense of justice to ever again ally himself to the shifting vagaries of official government service?

The odds were already stacked astronomically against one man pulling off what the Executioner intended inside Russia, and now it looked as if even that slim chance was about to be snuffed out.

And Hal Brognola, the one man trusted by Bolan, had no way of warning him in time.

KATRINA MOZZHECHKOV'S HEARTBEAT increased when she heard the steady footfalls of her jailers' boots marching down the corridor toward her cell.

She rose from the cement ledge that jutted out from the wall, the only place to sit.

Her cell in the basement of Lefortovo Prison was a cramped, dank, brick-walled square with a narrow high window in one wall, but she had been unable to stretch or jump high enough to look out of it during the time she had been imprisoned there.

She had lost track of time, though it was still dark outside the window. She could tell that much.

She pressed her back against the wall farthest from the door, wishing she had something, anything, to use as a weapon in case it was Kulik coming for her again, but of course there was nothing to fight with.

The twenty-five-watt bulb in the ceiling was too high to reach, to break and use to cut with, and in any event the bulb was encased in a wire mesh housing bolted to the ceiling.

She had heard horror stories about the "psychological cells" in Lefortovo, and this one was typical: an asphalt floor with a half inch of scummy, foul water, the maddening drip-drip-drip coming from some source she had been unable to ascertain.

The water was very cold, the heating valve located in the corridor outside the cell where only her guards had access to it. There was no latrine bucket, and many previous prisoners had relieved themselves upon the dirty floor or against murky walls.

The stench had at first threatened to gag her when she had been thrown in there, but she had fought to remain calm.

A spasm of fear quivered through her now.

The footfalls stopped outside her cell.

She had hoped they would pass her by. She could hear that she was not alone down in this black hole of misery. Moans and cries of suffering and desperation echoed weirdly through the underground maze of cells.

After running into the police net in Sokolniki Park, she had regained consciousness in the back of the police car driven by the bull-necked brute in uniform named, he had gruffly informed her, Sergeant Kulik. During the short drive, Kulik had leered at her in the rearview mirror. She had noticed that the inside of the patrol car's back doors did not have handles.

There had been no way to escape, nor had there been when Kulik had delivered her into the hands of the prison guards, who had accompanied them, each uniformed, robotlike guard grabbing one of her arms and half leading, half dragging her to the cell she was now in.

Kulik had followed Katrina and her guards down whitewashed corridors. She had felt the beast undressing her with his eyes every step of the way.

There had been no use trying to say anything to these men. The guards had worn AK-47s strapped over their shoulders, each guard loudly, repeatedly snapping the fingers of his right hand as they had led her deeper and deeper into the bowels of Lefortovo, the finger-snapping sounding odd to Katrina, like someone keeping the beat while listening to some popular tune. But she had quickly realized the snapping had had a more practical purpose.

Other prisoners were being escorted in either direction along the same corridor as they were led to or from interrogation, and the finger-snapping by all the guards would signal the approach of another prisoner.

She knew something of the methods of this madhouse. Dissident suspects were kept separate from one another at all costs. They were not even allowed to know who their fellow inmates were, so that when her guards had heard the snapping fingers of other guards coming from the opposite direction with some other unfortunate, Katrina's escorts had twisted her around to face the wall, smashing her nose brutally into it so as to divert her eyes from the person being led by.

This had happened twice, and on the second occasion she had felt Kulik's slavering breath against the back of her neck as the giant had pressed himself against her from behind, reaching down between her legs to paw at her roughly through her slacks.

She had cried out into the wall, but her guards had done nothing to stop Kulik, who had snickered and followed closer behind when the other guards and prisoner had passed. Then they had tossed her into her cell and had left her alone.

Her guards had left her alone, that is.

Not Kulik.

She heard a key turning in the heavy lock.

She stopped breathing for a moment, waiting with increasing panic to see who would enter. The guards, she hoped.

Kulik had visited her twice, alone, in the thirty minutes or so since she had been thrown in the cell. He had not touched her as he had had in the corridor. He hadn't touched her at all. He had stood there just inside the door, leering hungrily at her, nothing more. But it had been bad enough the way he had silently stripped her with his eyes, not speaking a word. Then he had let himself out of the cell…until he had come in again a few minutes later and done the same.

Part of her, most of her, trembled with terror, but a spark burned inside and would not let her give in to the growing desperation.

She knew Mack Bolan would not give in at a moment like this. She intended to emulate the spirit of the big American fighter who had passed through her life tonight like a lithe panther on the kill.

She could not stem her worry for him. She would give anything to know what had happened to that special fighting man after Kulik had knocked her unconscious in the park.

The cell door creaked inward on rusty hinges.

If Kulik touches me, I shall kill him, even if I have to tear his jugular open with my bare teeth, her mind screamed.

Two uniformed guards shouldered their hefty bulk inside the cell, grabbing her by each arm. They moved robotlike as before, dead-eyed, emotionless automatons, slaves of a slave state, she thought bitterly.

They led her from the cell.

They only stopped once, in a stairwell, to roughly press her face into the wall as another prisoner was guided down the stairs past them to his or her own cell.

Katrina heard pitiable whimpering but could not tell if it was man or woman, boy or girl, being escorted by other guards.

Her guards resumed dragging her up the stairs.

How can people be made to treat one another this way, she wondered, riding hard on her self-control to keep tears of frustration from her eyes. These guards, these young men, have mothers, childhoods... Fear makes them behave like this. And she well knew this same fear would make them deaf to any entreaties to their humanity. She moaned and realized she was half delirious from all she had been through.

Her guards halted at a door midway down the third-floor corridor. They opened the door, pitching Katrina bodily inside with force enough to send her to the floor, then slammed the door behind her and left.

Katrina landed on her hands and knees, bracing herself to look up through errant skeins of her hair at what, who, waited for her in this room.

She saw Kulik, and fear spasmed through her.

The hulking police sergeant stood in a position of supreme dominance, arms folded across his barrel chest, shiny black boots spread, squarely planted.

He stared down at her with a sneer of hate mingled with lust, the glare of fluorescent overheads reflecting from the patina of sweat beaded across his crew-cut head.

And yet Katrina sensed that this mountainous animal was dominant over her, but not over the other man in the room who sat cross-legged on the straight-backed chair in the center of the room, the one piece of furniture.

This man smoked a cigarette almost idly, though she saw clearly enough the interest that sparked in his eyes when she was tossed into the room.

She recognized him, too.

He was the one who had been in command in Sokolniki Park; the one who had ordered Kulik to strike her unconscious.

She rose slowly to her feet and stood, or tried to, facing them.

"I am Captain Anatoli Zuyenko of the Moscow Police," the seated man told her in clipped tones.

The gleam of his stare as his eyes traveled up and down the length of her body reminded her of Kulik. She shuddered, not in fear this time, but in revulsion, the hate she felt for these subhumans scorching every other emotion in her.

"What will you do to me now, Captain?" she asked, reborn steel in her voice. "I will tell you nothing. I will make you kill me. I don't know how I could live after being touched by feces like him." She jerked her head to indicate Kulik.

Zuyenko stood, smiling, a small smile that told Katrina he enjoyed her insolence. "We shall see, my dear." He motioned to the chair. "Kulik," he whispered.

Katrina started to back away but not quickly enough. Kulik grasped her upper arm to throw her into the vacated chair, retaining hold of her arm in a viselike grip. He swung his free hand around in a brutal backhanded slap. The inside of Katrina's head seemed to explode, the blow toppling her from the chair to her knees. Kulik did not release her. He laughed harshly, twisting her arm, causing her to scream out sharply once, then she bit her lip to stem the scream and felt blood trickle down her chin.

Kulik yanked her up roughly, righting her in the chair. Then he released her. Her head drooped forward, her chin resting on her chest. She saw droplets of blood from her split lip drip onto the pale green pajamalike prison uniform they had made her wear.

Her mind raced. *No! I will not be defeated.* She made herself look away from Kulik, who towered beside and slightly behind her, to Zuyenko, who stood facing her.

Both men chuckled at her humiliation.

"You see, my dear," Zuyenko purred almost pleasantly. "There is much we can still do to you."

"Then do it, and damn your soul to hell! I will tell you nothing!"

"Oh, I think you shall, Citizen Mozzhechkov. You see, I have been granted full authority to conduct this interrogation for the KGB. They, I, want to know what you were doing in Sokolniki Park this morning."

She forced herself to calm her mind, to think rationally. This is but the lowest echelon, she reminded herself. They know nothing about Mack Bolan or they would already be asking about him. Their superiors know of the Executioner's presence in Moscow, but not these oafs. If they had captured or killed Bolan in the park after she was apprehended, these sadists would know about it; the body would have been identified.

Her heart soared, and for a moment she forgot the pain, the humiliation, even the hate.

Mack is alive!

The Executioner had no way of knowing where she was. There was no chance of him arriving here before these ghouls did more to her, but the idea that he had made it safely out of Sokolniki Park gave her strength.

Katrina did not know why the big American had come to Moscow, why her group had been asked and sacrificed so much to help, but it had to be important, a vital matter.

She had seen Bolan in action in Afghanistan.

Her enemies, these slave masters who ruled from the Kremlin, were marked men, she knew, even if she would not live to see it.

"I will tell you nothing," she repeated to Zuyenko in a voice of quiet iron. "Do what you will."

10

The Executioner was togged for a hard-night hit. He was stripped down to the combat blacksuit he had worn beneath his regular clothes since his penetration of Russia had begun.

The combat suit, designed to his specifications, was skintight and covered thermal underwear.

The .44 AutoMag was nestled in its holster against a muscled right thigh, gunfighter style. The Beretta 93-R resided in its speed rig beneath his left arm near a sheathed combat knife.

The head weapon for this hit was a compact, silenced Uzi submachine gun, part of the contents of the attaché case supplied by Niktov. The Uzi hung by its shoulder strap, held close to Bolan's side.

Canvas pouches encircled his waist, loaded with extra ammo and grenades, also supplied by Niktov. A wire garrote and a lightweight array of hard-punch munitions completed his gear, none of it cumbersome.

The falling snow had not abated by the time he parked Tanya's Volvo on a street half a block from Lefortovo Prison. Moscow is nothing if not an efficient city. He had passed a dozen or more snowplow crews out in force even at this predawn hour, and by the time he had approached the vicinity of the prison the streets had been cleared of fallen snow, the traffic light enough so that the only delays he had encountered were occasional stoplights.

He left the car parked near an alley that connected with one of the streets leading to the intersection at the southwest corner of the stone walls of the prison. He positioned himself at the end of the alley, taking in what he could of the sprawling institution.

Lefortovo Prison looked impenetrable. Twenty-foot-high concrete walls, at least six feet thick, surrounded the prison. The walls were topped with curled strands of concertina wire and, Bolan guessed from his previous run-ins with such fortifications, the tops of those walls would be embedded with razor-sharp shards of glass.

Blockhouses sat on each corner where the walls met, visible from his position, and though he could see only the two nearest ones through the snow, he was willing to bet more such blockhouses would be perched on the opposite corners of the walls.

The eddying snow gathered intensity, making long-distance vision come and go despite the high-voltage lights mounted at intervals along the prison perimeter, especially around the iron gates built into an entrance, not the main one, near the southwest corner.

There would be plenty of firepower in each of those blockhouses, to say nothing of the gatehouse he glimpsed at the southwest entrance.

Normally on a wintertime night hit like this, he would have worn the white model of his combat outfit, but he had traveled light for this mission and, under the circumstances, he knew the blacksuit would be sufficient, perhaps preferable once he got inside.

The snow was his friend, not only because the falling white stuff would erase his footprints as soon as he made them, but also because the snow and the frigid air would stack some more odds in his favor. Those in the block-houses would most likely be unable to see him down here any more than he could see them, and the outside guards would have their collars wrapped around them to shield them from the elements. This would make things easier for him, too.

Of course, in a case like this *easy* was a relative term, Bolan realized grimly, but he had another ally—the pre-dawn hour, the best possible time for an action such as the one he was about to undertake. After a night, or at least several hours of guard duty, the average sentry's boredom and tiredness begin to work on him, and it would work better for Bolan's purpose with a setup like this. The guards and sentries of Lefortovo were not de-fending a military position; they would hardly be on guard against anyone trying to break *in*.

Bolan didn't kid himself that this would be a walk in the park. He estimated dawn to be less than twenty minutes away. The eastern horizon would have already been smudged with the gray of false dawn if not for the veils of blowing snow, but once the sun rose Bolan knew the snow would only intensify the light.

He also knew that a penetration of Lefortovo by force was out of the question. Even with the hour and the ele-ments on his side, he could hardly take on the prison's entire security firepower from the outside. He might well have to bust out that way, but as for breaking inside those walls, the best way could only be a soft probe.

The watcher in snowy shadows discerned the rumble of a heavy vehicle approaching through the city streets an instant before headlight beams swung into the street along the wall. A truck grumbled toward him in the direction of the entrance at the other end of the block, the truck making slow progress in the snow.

Bolan crouched back farther into the alley so that the headlights would not pick him out for the prison sentries. He made out the details of the truck as it came closer, the driver downshifting in preparation for stopping at the southwest gate.

A nonmilitary vehicle—a refrigerated delivery truck probably, Bolan reasoned, as it approached the mouth of the alley to deliver food for the guards and administrators of Lefortovo.

There would be no meat or vegetables for the inmates. In the Soviet gulag, it's gruel for breakfast, gruel for lunch and gruel for dinner. This would be a regular, scheduled delivery, and for that reason the guards would be lax in searching it.

Bolan prepared to pounce.

The truck rumbled past the alley, the driver holding the speed down to no more than ten miles per hour as the truck drew closer to the entrance.

He made his move just after the high cab of the truck passed his position, darting out from the alley with a leap that latched him onto the back of the truck like a spider to a wall. He scrambled, using the back sliding door handle of the truck for support and grip, then lowered himself to the underside of the truck.

The street adjacent to the prison remained otherwise deserted, since there were no storefronts along here for security reasons, but also because Muscovites probably shunned prison walls that represented all the fear their leaders used to make them toe the line.

No one saw him.

The driver commenced braking as the truck approached the heavy iron gate. The slow pace meant Bolan was in no danger of bodily injury. The blowing snow shielded him from the guards' view, even if they had been interested in looking under a truck they probably saw at this time every other morning or so.

The snow, kicked up by the truck's rear tires, glued itself to the undercarriage. Bolan's bare fingers grew numb as he pressed his belly up flush against the truck, his grip starting to loosen, his palms slipping on the ice formed along every available handhold.

The truck braked to a complete stop.

Bolan, coated now with a thin dusting of snow kicked up by the tires, released one hand at a time, holding on as well as he could with his other, yanking himself up for a better grip, doing the same with his other hand, gaining a better hold.

He paid close attention to what he could see and hear from his perch beneath the truck. A sentry came out of the gatehouse and glanced routinely at the orders authorizing the delivery truck's access to the grounds.

"Damn snow," the driver grumbled. "I thought we'd seen the last of it until fall."

The sentry snorted. The rustle of paper told Bolan the guard was handing the orders back to the man in the cab.

"If it's bad, it will happen," the sentry philoso-phized. "All right, move on through. And tell the cook to save some for us."

The sentry stepped back from the truck and made a hand signal to two men in the guardhouse just inside the gate.

Weapon barrels poked out through slots in the bullet-proof window of the guardhouse, but from his angle Bolan could see the sentries inside were not behind those rifles. He had correctly gauged their response to the truck's arrival. The sentries were barely interested in the truck.

At the outside guard's signal, someone activated a mechanism that made a heavy-duty iron grille gate slide back into the wall. The truck began to move through the entrance, and Bolan held on to the truck's underside with rapidly numbing fingers. The gate made a whir-ring sound and a *clang* that echoed as the vehicle rolled through a slanting, enclosed entranceway just inside the gate.

Bolan retained his position as the driver geared down to negotiate a slope into what Bolan discerned to be a courtyard. He lowered his head slightly, holding fast to the icy underside of the vehicle.

As the truck angled to the right, he made out the tow-ering, featureless stone faces of the buildings inside Le-fortovo. He paid special attention to what he could see of the building in the southwest corner, the building where Tanya had told him he would find Katrina.

The prison compound was constructed around a square, and there appeared to be any number of small alleyways and shadowed areas where the high intensity lights did not reach and the blowing snow would obstruct the guards' vision from much of the courtyard.

The truck rumbled past Building D where Katrina was held.

Bolan clearly saw enough at this range to note one significant difference between Building D and the other cellblocks and administrative buildings: there was an extra heavy concentration of sentries around the building where Tanya had told him two sadists named Zuyenko and Kulik would be interrogating his friend.

Besides six uniformed prison guards at each of the building's three entrances, there was a BTR-40 armored car, like the one the Moscow cops had used in the park, complete with 7.62 mm SGMG submachine gun in the turret, parked dead center in front of Building D.

The delivery truck passed so close to the armored car that Bolan caught a few words of exchange among three soldiers manning the BTR-40, the conversation concerning the timeless soldier's lament of duty in inclement weather.

The truck wheeled on past another of the buildings, finally drawing to a halt in front of the third building in from the gate.

Bolan clearly noted that, while he could discern the very presence of guards and a smattering of Russian soldiers, even some civilian and plainclothes office workers just showing up for work, none of the other buildings he could see boasted anything near the security measures around Building D.

The truck driver cut the engine and lights. Bolan heard him debark from the cab. The driver strode through the falling snow toward the front entrance of the building.

Bolan did not hear the man shut the truck cab's door, which told Bolan he would be back within seconds. This would be the mess hall for prison personnel, the driver heading inside so that the cook or whoever was in charge could send out a detail to unload the truck, most likely while the driver stayed warm in the cab.

Bolan dropped from the underside of the truck, pushing out from beneath the vehicle the instant he touched ground, quickly and noiselessly traversing the twenty meters separating the truck from the next building, the one between the mess hall and Building D.

He darted along the length of the walkway, barely noticing the nippy bite of wind-lashed snow wrapping the exposed skin of his face and hands in its prickly embrace. He reached the far end of the paved path just as he heard men's voices and the shuffling of unenthusiastic feet.

The front door of the building opened, and a moment later he heard the delivery truck backing into the opposite end of the areaway. He dodged around the corner to the rear of the next building in line before anyone noticed movement other than snow flurries.

The men began unloading the truck back there, and Bolan knew he had nothing to be concerned about from that direction. He crouched for a moment at the base of the building, unlooping the specially designed climbing rope from its notch on his belt, another gift from Niktov.

He estimated forty meters or so from the rear of these buildings to the prison wall that loomed up out of sight into the shroud of falling and blowing snow. It reminded him of the side of a sheer cliff disappearing into clouds.

There would be guards patrolling a walkway up there just inside the wall, but if he couldn't see them they probably couldn't see him either, and anyway, he reasoned, he had no choice in what he was about to do.

He couldn't assault Building D head-on. He had to find Katrina before the fireworks began. If he didn't, he would risk not reaching her at all, or he might find her dead. He had to get inside that building covertly, if at all possible. Then he could go to work.

He moved down the length of the middle building, then darted across another areaway, unspotted by the sentries at the side entrance midway down. He paused at the base of the blind side of Building D, which had no entranceway or ground-floor windows, and so there were no sentries posted there.

He stepped away from the building and twirled the lightweight rope with the metal three-pronged mountain climbing hook attached to it. He judged the distance to a dark, unbarred fourth-floor window ledge, then let the hook fly. The erratic gusts of wind higher up along the building's face threw off the rope and its grapnel.

He tried a second time, senses constantly alert. The snow muffled and distorted the sounds of his activity, and this time the mountain climbing prongs caught on the window ledge. Bolan got a firm grip on the rope, lifted one booted foot at a time to brace himself against the stone wall, then began climbing hand over hand up the face of the building.

He stopped before reaching even the second-story window, his peripheral vision detecting three forms emerging from the snow—three prison guards armed with shoulder-strapped AK-47 assault rifles. The trio was either a scheduled patrol or simply three guys ducking out back for a smoke, possibly a hashish break, currently a big favorite in Russia's government services.

The only thing that mattered to Bolan was that the soldiers not see him. He thought of what could be happening to Katrina at this moment and hated like hell having to hold his position suspended there against the building a few feet above the soldiers' heads.

It looked as if they would stroll by below without noticing him, heading in the direction of the mess hall. Then one of the soldiers happened to glance upward as if at the elements. He saw Bolan.

The soldier's eyes and mouth flew open to sound a surprised alarm when he saw the figure in black suspended against the building. The man started to say something to his comrades who had already started to look up in Bolan's direction from the startled look on their companion's face.

Bolan propelled himself into a leap down at them, feet first, before any of the three could utter a sound or track their weapons around and up at the black-clad blur powerhousing down upon them.

The soldiers on either side of the guy who had seen Bolan broke the Executioner's fall when the heels of Bolan's boots caught each man in the forehead hard enough to smash skull bone backward into brain matter, killing both prison guards instantly.

The momentum of Bolan's fall carried him through into a somersault. He came out of it in a smooth roll in time to see the third guard swing his rifle around on him, the man's features wild with panic at the sight of his two fallen comrades.

Bolan moved in at full speed, arcing his foot up in a high martial arts kick that knocked the AK-47 from the soldier's grip. Then he twisted around in a smooth recovery to spear his stiffened right hand straight at the guard's throat, feeling the blow crush the guard's larynx. To finish him off, Bolan chopped his left hand down sharply to break the man's neck and send him collapsing down to fall upon the bodies of the first two.

He considered for an instant what to do about the three corpses, but there seemed nothing he could do except leave them where they had fallen. The unloading of the delivery truck meant he couldn't hide the stiffs between the two buildings. The back of this building was as sheer as the front and the other structures. There wasn't even a doorway where Bolan could stash the bodies. Besides, he told himself, this hit would get hot within the next minute or two. He would just have to hope the bodies weren't discovered during that time.

He regripped the dangling rope with both hands, then braced himself again against the wall and started climbing. It was a difficult climb because his feet kept sliding on the snowy brick, but he made it to the unbarred window within a few seconds and saw that the other windows on this level were also unbarred. That made this an administration building, which meant workers would be showing up in their offices at any second.

He held tight to the rope looped around one wrist. With the other gloved hand, he worked for a few moments in an attempt to ease the window up, finding that it was locked from the inside. He made a fist and delivered a short punch to one of the windowpanes, striking the glass only with the force necessary to shatter the one pane. The sound of the glass tinkling to the carpeted floor inside was entirely lost to Bolan's own ears as the wind howled between the buildings and the nearby wall. He hoped the sound would be equally muffled to anyone inside the building.

Maintaining his left-handed grip on the rope, he reached in through the smashed windowpane and felt around a bit before he located the window latch. He twisted the latch, pulled his arm out and, pressing his fingers against one of the remaining panes of glass, pushed up at the same time. The window rolled upward on its runners.

He returned both hands to grip the rope and tug himself up and over the window ledge, easing himself inside the building. He pulled the rope up after him and pulled down the window. He looped the rope back on his belt and swung the silenced Uzi around into firing position, making a quick scan of the large office of several desks and typewriters and file cabinets.

He started toward the office door to let himself out.

At that precise moment a key turned in the lock of the office door.

Bolan hurried to the wall next to the door, pressing his back against it, bringing up the Uzi.

The door opened, and a middle-aged woman stepped in. She reached for the light switch, the first of the civilian office workers showing up. She didn't see Bolan, who had positioned himself behind the door.

He watched her feeling for the light switch, knowing the instant she turned it on she would see the shards of glass strewn on the carpet beneath the window, whereupon she would surely raise an alarm. He could not allow that.

He moved in before the woman knew it, delivering a crisp punch with the Uzi to the base of her neck, this time not a killing blow but with enough strength to render her unconscious.

The woman emitted a soft sigh, and her knees buckled. She started to fall. Bolan closed in, catching her hefty bulk before she could collapse. He slipped his arms beneath hers and positioned her behind a desk. He stretched her out on the floor, then hurried out of the office, knowing the time spent dealing with the woman would only buy him a few minutes at most.

Secretaries and other clerical help who worked the desks in the office would no doubt show up for work anytime now. They would see the glass, they would find their unconscious co-worker and they would sound the alarm. But Bolan saw no alternative to the way he had dealt with the woman. He did not want to kill a Russian civilian who just happened to be in the wrong place at the wrong time. He did not want innocent blood on his hands.

He left the office and looked up and down a corridor that ran the length of the building, a hallway lined with the closed doors of other offices. An elevator at the opposite end of the hall would be the means by which the employees came up, since a metal door, closer to Bolan at his end of the corridor, bore a stenciled Emergency Exit Only in Cyrillic script.

He moved to the metal door, pushed it and found the door locked as he had half expected. He stepped back and triggered off a short burst at the lock.

Nine-millimeter slugs destroyed the lock, the noise of the silenced burst sounding like little more than an impolite burp, drowned out as Bolan followed through with a mighty kick that sent the metal door slapping inward.

He came through the doorway in a forward dive that sent him belly flat onto the cement of the fourth-floor landing, fire stairs zigzagging up and down the shaft.

Three uniformed prison guards positioned on the next landing down whirled as one, eyes and mouths widening in surprise.

They pushed away from one another, starting to swing weapons up at an attacker they could not see in the dim lighting of the stairwell.

The Executioner's Uzi unleashed an extended burst down the stairs, spraying brick walls with modern art designs of splattering blood, a withering hail of projectiles shredding the guards.

Bolan raced down the stairs toward a door that matched the one he had just come through except that this door led to the third floor where he hoped he would find Katrina Mozzhechkov before the savages did anything to her....

11

Bolan knew his only chances were the element of surprise and the fact that the beefed-up security around Building D was for the most part on the outside. They obviously did not expect a soft probe and had certainly not expected the prober to actually get inside the building.

He inched open the stairwell door to the third-floor corridor and peered out. Down the hallway two prison sentries stood guard on either side of the third door. Behind that door was where Tanya had told Bolan he would find Katrina.

These guards would be standard, but in that moment he wondered again about the tripled manpower below, outside the building, as if they were ready and waiting for the Executioner to strike....

He kneed the stairwell door open and flew into the corridor, hitting the floor on his stomach. He tracked up the Uzi on the two sentries, hoping he would be able to take them out as soundlessly as he had those in the stairwell and outside, keeping his presence undetected by any except the dead and one unconscious secretary.

The startled guards jerked away from the wall to a side-by-side position, trying to track their rifles in Bolan's direction.

He coaxed a burst from the Uzi, and it riddled the guy on the right. The impact of the slugs mule-kicked the man backward into the wall. His knees folded and he fell.

Bolan tracked the Uzi on sentry number two, and the Uzi jammed.

The guard, who had fully expected to die in that second, saw his chance and fell forward to a prone position, triggering off a booming round from his AK-47 that thundered in the confines of the hallway, sending a heavy projectile singing too close for comfort past Bolan's ear.

Bolan rolled over once to his left, unholstering the .44 AutoMag, putting himself out of the guard's line of fire.

The man hammered off another round that pulverized a portion of the wall behind where Bolan had been an eye blink before, then the prison guard became headless as Big Thunder roared, the slug pitching the guy into an almost physically impossible flip-flop onto his back.

Bolan bolted off the floor, pausing in a crouch as the door the guards had been watching opened.

A mountainous hulk in a police uniform stuck his head and an arm out of the door in Bolan's direction.

Kulik.

Bolan triggered another round from the AutoMag, the bullet taking of the sadist's gun hand, spinning juicy pulp and Kulik's pistol across the hall.

The cop screamed and stumbled into the hallway, falling to his knees, squeezing the pulsating stump with his good hand, blindly shrieking at the top of his lungs.

Bolan drew this guy's head away, too, then rushed the open doorway, knowing the numbers were all used up on this hit. The gunfire would bring an immediate reaction from the forces outside and those in the building.

He came through the doorway into the "interrogation room" just as Captain Zuyenko managed to dart behind a chair, the only piece of furniture in the room. The Soviet cop grabbed for a shoulder-holstered pistol with his right hand and wrapped his left arm around the throat of Katrina Mozzhechkov; both Zuyenko and Katrina looking very surprised at Bolan's presence here.

Bolan came in, his right arm extended, the stainless-steel barrel of Big Thunder an extension of the steady arm and eye behind it.

At that same moment the police officer yanked Katrina back flush against him, raising the barrel of his gun toward her temple.

Katrina was held too tightly in Zuyenko's grip for her to struggle. Her face appeared bruised where she had been slapped repeatedly prior to Bolan's appearance, but she wore her prison uniform in place; they had not graduated to the serious interrogation yet.

Zuyenko's face was bright with nervous sweat. "Drop your weapon or I kill her," he snarled at the figure in black in the doorway.

Bolan squeezed off a round from the AutoMag, and 240 grains of destruction shattered the hand holding the pistol at Katrina's head, peppering the cop's face with bone and gristle. The boattail slug continued on its relentless path of destruction, drilling Zuyenko's throat and most of the back of his skull, the impact tossing his corpse away from Katrina as the bullet's exit wound erupted in a fountain of spewing gore.

Bolan lowered Big Thunder.

"That guy saw too many movies," he said as he came in to lend Katrina a hand.

She didn't look too bad despite her ordeal. Shaken mostly, discernible in a tremulous lower lip, but she also looked capable of holding herself together in this or any other crisis. Some woman.

He extended an arm.

Katrina came to him.

"Do you know who I am?" Bolan asked her.

The life mask did not fool her.

"I may not know your face, but I certainly recognize your methods. Besides, no one has eyes like yours, Mack Bolan." She leaned against him as they moved to the door away from the remains of Zuyenko. "Thank God," she shuddered into his shoulder. "I wanted to die. In another minute they said they were going to..."

Her words tapered off raggedly.

They reached the door.

"Can you make it?" Bolan asked. "Do you want me to carry you?"

"N-no, I can make it."

He drew the Beretta from its shoulder holster and handed it to her. "Take this."

She took it. He rapidly showed her how to switch the 93-R from single fire to 3-shot mode.

"I understand," she said. "What now?"

"Stay with me."

He moved out from the doorway.

Katrina stayed close.

He hurried to one of the dead sentries in the hallway, holstered Big Thunder and grabbed the dead man's AK, the Soviet counterpart of the M-16, and some spare ammo clips that he stuck in his belt.

Katrina positioned herself just behind him while he did this, her back to him, covering his blind side, aiming the Beretta in a two-handed shooter's stance down the opposite end of the hallway, her legs firmly planted, bent slightly, every sign of shakiness gone.

Then time ran out.

The stairwell doorways at both ends of the corridor flew open, disgorging half a dozen rifle-toting prison guards who charged blindly from where they had been positioned outside around the building, responding to the gunfire from up here.

Bolan and Katrina opened fire in either direction.

Katrina's Beretta stuttered a 3-round burst.

Two of the guards at her end of the hallway crumpled amid torrents of blood. Four other men coming close on their heels immediately reversed themselves at first sight of the dying. They dived back into the safety of the stairwell.

Bolan kept his trigger finger squeezing out nearly half a clip of death that sliced apart five Russians at his end of the corridor before any of them could bring up their rifles into firing position.

"This way," Bolan instructed Katrina.

He led the way down the hall in the opposite direction from which he had come, his mind focusing on what would be happening outside at this minute.

The Executioner had been cruising the hellgrounds long enough to know that the force he had seen clustered around each of this building's entrances would be dispersing by now. He was betting that half of the guards would be ordered to remain at each of those entrances while the officers in charge sent the rest to encircle the building. And others would be dispatched to where Zuyenko and Kulik had been interrogating Katrina.

Those circling the building outside would find three dead men, bringing concentration of activity. So for this reason Bolan headed for the opposite end of the building, formulating strategy as he went.

He and the woman reached the end of the hallway where the five Soviets lay dead.

He kicked open an office door and nodded Katrina on through.

She hustled into the dark office.

The metal door to the stairwell at the other end of the hall disgorged the remaining guards who now thought they had a chance.

Bolan braced himself for the recoil and emptied the rest of the AK-47's clip down the length of the hallway before any of the jerks could trigger a shot. The assault rifle's blast shook plaster from the ceiling and walls. The four men danced around under the impact, uniforms rippling as the slugs drilled on through, stitching the guards like a giant sewing machine until Bolan released the AK's trigger and the four perforated bodies collapsed on top of one another.

He stepped into the office after Katrina, kicking the door shut behind him and locking it.

That wouldn't hold the security off the scent for very long. The stairwells and elevator would already be full of men pounding up in the direction of the third floor, but the closed office door, matching all the other closed doors lining this hallway, this slaughterhouse full of corpses, would slow them down for a minute or so at least.

Bolan glanced at Katrina.

She caught the glance and smiled back bravely. She held the Beretta like a master.

He slammed a fresh clip into the AK-47 and rushed across to the single window of the office. He reached the window and stood alongside it to look out and down.

The window was directly above the side doorway. Bolan nodded to no one in particular. He had read their security response correctly.

Three soldiers with Kalashnikovs stood in a tight half circle around the entrance, rifles fanning the blowing snow, which had whipped up heavier during the time that Bolan had been inside the building.

The prison compound, or what Bolan could see of it from the window, crackled with activity. A klaxon siren moaned eerily in the half-light, and the first gray of dawn cut through the eddying clouds of snow. Most of the activity came from in front of the building.

He smashed out the window glass with the barrel of the AK-47 and began squeezing the trigger before the sound of shattering glass could warn the three below. Blazing lead pitched them onto their faces. The snow beneath them began to turn into spreading crimson designs that rapidly disappeared as new snow covered the stains and the bodies.

Bolan unhitched the climbing rope he had used to enter Building D. He slung the AK over his shoulder and unholstered Big Thunder. He crawled out on the window ledge and looked back at Katrina, who joined him at the window.

"The rope is treated," he told her. "Just slide down. It won't burn. I'll cover you." He kicked off and rode the rope down, but when he was only halfway to the ground two sentries came dashing around the rear of the building.

They saw Bolan.

Bolan triggered the AutoMag from his right fist as he gripped the rope with his left. He touched ground at the same instant as two dead guards.

He stepped away from the building, holstered the AutoMag and swung the AK-47 around.

Katrina lifted one shapely leg, then the other over the window ledge and started to follow Bolan down.

There came a chatter of automatic rifle fire. A line of bullet holes pockmarked the bricks near Katrina's head.

Bolan swung the AK around, looking for a human target, unable to pinpoint the source of fire.

Katrina set down on the ground at his side, unhurt.

Bolan immediately took off along the side of the building toward the front, not pausing to retrieve the pronged climbing device.

Katrina stayed right behind him.

They gained the corner of the building. He motioned Katrina to stay close.

He chanced a one-eyed peek around the corner at the scene in front of the building.

The three guards he expected to see stood just as the three at the first entrance had, their backs to the building, attention and rifles alert but in the wrong direction.

The BTR-40 sat where he had seen it on the way in, one of the two men sitting behind the steering wheel, the other visible in the swirling snow where he stood partially exposed behind the submachine gun mounted in the turret.

A security officer led nine rifle-carrying guards on the run into Building D through the main entrance.

The three posted guards and the men in the armored vehicle stayed put.

Automatic gunfire opened up from nearby. A short line of slugs geysered snow less than twelve inches from where Bolan and Katrina stood.

Katrina spotted the source of fire and swung the Beretta 93-R up into another two-handed firing posture. She unleashed a 3-shot burst that cut off the automatic fire.

A sentry toppled from the walkway along the wall just behind Building D.

"Good shooting," Bolan complimented, handing her a fresh clip for the pistol.

She smoothly palmed the magazine into the 93-R. "We'll never make it!" she said.

Bolan unhooked a grenade from his combat webbing. "Let's try."

He pulled the pin from the grenade, stepped away from the building, exposing only enough of himself necessary to take aim, and tossed the grenade in an accurate overhand pitch in the direction of the BTR-40.

He stepped back closer to the building, ramming out another lengthy burst from the AK, riding the recoil of the rifle as it spat fire, spent shell casings ejecting in a smoking stream to drop and sizzle in the snow.

The three troopers positioned at the main entrance were blown sideways off their feet and deposited willy-nilly as if tossed about by a tornado.

Then the Executioner's peripheral vision glimpsed the scene at the armored car.

The grenade plopped on target into the turret where the machine gunner saw it clank down between his feet. The guy behind the steering wheel spotted Bolan but had no time to react.

The machine gunner had enough time to scream, a cry of pure terror swallowed up by the blast of the grenade a second after Bolan put the corner of the building between himself and the vehicle.

The explosion, quieter than usual because of the density of falling snow, came as Bolan fed a fresh clip into his AK.

Snow swirled and gusted through the compound, but the creeping light of dawn improved visibility by the minute.

Two soldiers in the courtyard saw Bolan and Katrina and tracked their rifles in the direction of the combat-garbed man and the escaped prisoner.

Bolan and Katrina moved away from each other, Bolan triggering a short burst from the AK, kicking one of the soldiers back into his personal doomsday before he could fire a shot.

The second soldier squeezed off a burst that, in his excitement, went high, studding the brick above and behind Bolan.

Katrina's answering fire missed the soldier.

Bolan shifted his rifle slightly and blasted the guy, who tumbled backward to join his dead buddy in the snow.

Bolan turned to Katrina. "Stay put until I signal you to come."

She nodded, her alert, vigilant eyes panning the scene for more danger, more targets.

Bolan sprinted from the building toward the BTR-40 before the echoes of rifle fire or the blast of the grenade receded between the towering walls of Lefortovo.

Activity in the courtyard had lessened, sentries in the blockhouses and catwalks along the wall maintaining their positions, unable to do anything but listen to the gunfire, their visibility severely limited by the full-fledged snowstorm pounding the city.

Most other available manpower had already been dispatched into Building D, or to quiet prisoners throughout the prison whom Bolan could vaguely hear raising hell in every cellblock.

Attention would already be drawn to the grenade blast.

Bolan reached the BTR-40, passing the sprawled corpses of the three sentries he had taken out in front of the main entrance of Building D.

All that remained of the machine gunner who had been standing in the back of the armored car was the lower part of his torso. It was draped across the metal plating of the vehicle. The rest of him, not protected by the armor, looked as if it had been hacked away with a dull chainsaw—dark, gruesome and pulsating.

The man's head had rolled across like a bloody basketball against the first step of Building D's entrance, leaving a long red trail behind it across the snow.

The driver inside the vehicle, protected from shrapnel by the bulletproof glass, twisted the ignition key.

The BTR-40 rumbled to life.

The driver hurriedly started to slip the vehicle into gear to get away, turning a panic-stricken face on the Executioner.

Bolan leaped onto the running board and yanked the door open before the driver thought to lock it.

The vehicle popped into gear and jerked forward in the direction of the incline, moving toward the closed iron gate.

Bolan gripped the frame of the truck with one arm for support. The jarring movement of the vehicle almost tumbled him to the snow. He reached inside with his other hand before the vehicle had rolled a dozen meters, grasping the driver behind his collar, tossing him out of the vehicle.

Bolan slid in behind the wheel in one smooth movement, regaining control of the slow-moving truck with his left hand on the wheel. With his right fist, he aimed the AK-47 across his chest and out the open, flapping door of the vehicle at the driver. He had landed on his back in the snow and was struggling to his feet, grasping for a holstered side arm. Bolan let loose a stinger that drilled the man through the heart.

The Executioner braked the vehicle, angling the truck's nose against the stone wall seven or eight meters short of the gate in such a way that the truck halted with its armored plating blocking Bolan from view and, more importantly, from the line of fire of most of the court-yard and those at the nearest blockhouse. He rushed to the door of the guardhouse.

The sentries inside were trying to twist their machine guns, mounted behind bulletproof glass, in Bolan's direction, but he was too close to them as he pressed himself flush against the wall.

One of the sentries let loose a burst, but all it did was send a stream of bullets singing off the armor plating of the BTR-40.

Bolan reached the door to the guardhouse and found it locked. He stayed against the wall, aimed his AK and fired a short burst that blew the locked door off its hinges. Then he plucked another grenade from his web-bing.

Shouts and rifle fire erupted in his direction from in-side the guardhouse built into the wall, but he was po-sitioned at such an angle that the hail of slugs pouring out of the doorway came nowhere near him. Without exposing himself to those trapped inside, he lobbed the grenade and pressed himself against the wall away from the door.

Katrina stood where he had left her, trading shots with two prison guards who had come out of the main en-trance of Building D in response to the action in front. She dropped one of the men, then ran out of ammuni-tion, and while she reloaded a few more prison guards snaked their way out of the entrance to cautiously ad-vance in her direction, though she had ducked out of their sight.

Bolan squeezed off leaden death across the distance, pinning three of the men to the wall before they collapsed into the snow, while the others made a quick withdrawal.

The grenade detonated inside the guardhouse, and the bulletproof glass became opaque with globs of blood and billowing smoke.

Bolan signaled with his arm for Katrina to leave her position and join him.

She left the cover of her corner of the building, jogging as fast as she could across the distance separating her from Bolan.

Machine-gun fire opened up from the blockhouse nearest Bolan. Slugs geysered more snow in a path toward Katrina.

She saw it coming and tried to dodge sideways. She tripped face first into the snow, the line of gunfire rapidly closing in on her.

Bolan stepped out from the wall alongside the guardhouse. His AK stammered a mean burst at the blockhouse.

The firing from up there ceased abruptly.

He dodged back into cover of the stone arches of the gateway as the gunner up there opened fire vainly on Bolan. Bolan pumped his last clip into the AK-47, watching with relief as Katrina pushed herself to her feet from the ground and zigzagged the rest of the way while he drew fire from the blockhouse, slugs spanging harmlessly off the BTR-40.

Gutsy Katrina even plugged off a couple of 3-shot bursts from the Beretta at the blockhouse before she reached Bolan's side.

"Into the truck," he told her. "Keep down!"

She did as Bolan ordered, and he darted inside the guardhouse. Through the mess of exploded bodies and drifting smoke he saw what was left of the console beneath the window. He quickly spotted the lever designated as the one that operated the gate. He threw the handle and ran back out to the truck.

The prison courtyard roared with violence, every bit of it aimed at the BTR-40, guards advancing on it from all over the compound, firing as they ran.

Bolan paused only long enough to empty the AK's last clip at several soldiers running in his direction from Building D. He did not wait to see how many fell. He tossed away the useless weapon.

The gate whirred open.

The Executioner threw himself behind the steering wheel of the BTR-40, seeing Katrina crouched low, as he had told her, though she held the Beretta ready.

As hundreds of bullets poured at and bounced off the armored vehicle, Bolan backed away from the wall, slammed into gear, catapulted the BTR-40 out through the open gate and two-wheeled into the snowy street in the new light of day.

The Executioner gunned the vehicle down the street at full speed away from Lefortovo.

12

0630 hours.

Katrina sat wrapped in a blanket in the front passenger seat of the Volvo, watching through the windshield as Mack Bolan, inside a telephone kiosk, spoke to someone after dialing the number Katrina had recited to him.

The falling snow had ceased. The city, blanketed in white, sparkled glaringly beneath a sunlit, cloudless blue sky, while passersby, their breath clouded before their faces in the brittle chill, bustled around the Volvo.

Katrina pulled the blanket tighter about herself, checking to make sure none of her prison uniform showed through the folds of the blanket. No one passing the car paid her the slightest bit of attention.

Trollies, automotive sounds, the audible crunching of hundreds of feet on the snowy sidewalk and occasional snatches of people's conversations from outside the car window filled her head, completing the reviving process from the nearly delirious state of captivity.

Her return to her senses had been sparked when she had seen Mack Bolan step into the interrogation room in Building D to rescue her from the cruelties of Zuyenko and Kulik.

She had recognized Bolan instantly, even though he had worn the latex mask and mustache. From the moment the fighting American had appeared in the doorway of the room and had handed her his Beretta, Katrina had felt herself rejuvenated with a vengeance that had spurred her during their escape from Lefortovo.

Bolan had driven the hijacked armored car to within less than a block of the prison walls, far enough away to be out of sight of the prison, and as daylight had etched the Moscow skyline and the snowstorm had cleared, the Executioner and Katrina had raced into the waiting Volvo, and Bolan had driven them away from there.

At first he had driven them through the streets with no particular destination in mind, merely putting distance between the Volvo and the prison, detouring up this street and that, in one direction and then the other.

She and Bolan had not exchanged words during that time, and she had felt herself almost succumbing to the aftershock of what had happened, not only of her capture but of the terrifying escape when she had been forced to take human lives . . . to witness so much.

Bolan, driving the Volvo, his eyes constantly shifting between the rearview and side mirrors and everything on the busy streets around them, had brought her back from the edge of shock and hysteria with the calm sureness of his firm voice.

"Katrina, you'll have to tell me where you want to go. I have to leave you. I have other work. It can't wait."

She had known she was all right again when she had felt herself smiling at what he had said.

"We have to stop meeting this way," she had chuckled. "Is that not a cliché of your American love stories?"

The icy eyes behind the wheel had softened. "That's the cliché, all right. And yeah, Katrina, let's meet some other time. Some better circumstances."

Before she knew it, she had asked, "Soon?"

"Yes. Soon. But right now—"

"I have friends in the movement," she had told him. "They live nearby. It would not be safe for us to go to their home, but they will come get me."

"That will have to do," he had growled. "Your people must be holding their breath to find out what's happened to you. And to me."

She had given him the phone number of her friends, and he appeared to be speaking to them now from inside the kiosk as she watched him from the Volvo.

He had rapidly donned Russian-cut civilian clothes in the car immediately after abandoning the armored car used in their escape. As far as she could tell, no one appeared to be paying any attention to the big, broad-shouldered man making the phone call, nor to the blanket-bundled woman in the car waiting for him to finish. And in a city with one or more KGB agents posted on practically every street corner, no one was safe, least of all two people who had just escaped from a maximum security prison, slaying scores of prison guards and Soviet soldiers in the process!

A police car appeared from behind, slowly cruising through the early-morning rush hour traffic of the thoroughfare. She noted that Bolan saw the police car, but he continued talking into the phone.

She gripped the Beretta in her right hand more tightly beneath the blanket, staring straight ahead but watching the police cruiser pass, her palm and index finger sweaty around the butt and trigger of the Beretta despite the chill of the air. If they noticed her at all, she hoped, perhaps they would think that she was wrapped in a blanket because the car heater had broken down. Unless they had a description of her.

The police cruiser continued past without slowing and disappeared into the forward flow of traffic. Katrina looked back at the phone kiosk. She saw Bolan replace the receiver and approach the Volvo. He got in behind the steering wheel.

"Your friends say they'll be here within three minutes. They'll pull up beside us and you can slip from this car into theirs. I doubt it will attract attention if we work it right."

She returned the Beretta to him when they were sure that no passersby would notice.

"I wish to thank you for all you have done—for bringing me to this neighborhood and for making that phone call . . . for everything."

He took the Beretta and holstered it beneath his jacket. "You did more than your part, Katrina. Will you be safe now?"

"No one who carries thoughts of their own is safe in Russia," she replied. She slipped a folded piece of paper into his hand. "This is the address of where I will be today, all day, until it is night when they will smuggle me out of the city."

He accepted the piece of paper, glanced at it and folded it again. He struck a match, held the piece of paper and burned it, dropping it into the dashboard tray where it became ash.

"I've memorized it. I may not survive what comes next."

"Please don't say that—"

"If I'm taken prisoner, or if they search my body, I don't want a piece of paper to lead them to you."

"What *does* come next?" she asked. "For you, I mean?"

"I can't tell you that. I'm sorry."

"I understand," she said, nodding. "It's just that I feel such relief at this moment, at being here alone with you this close. I feel relief to have escaped, of course. Now I shall have to leave Russia to fight them from the outside. They will not rest until they have found me, and if I stay they will be sure to find me sooner or later. There is no escape in my country. But I feel relief to know you are alive, Mack. The world needs you so. I had feared you were slain at Sokolniki Park. I thank God you made it out of there alive. And the woman, Zara?"

"She didn't make it."

"I'm sorry."

He appeared to be aware of everything outside around the Volvo while he gave his attention to her at the same time, but he broke eye contact with her when a vehicle glided to a stop in the parking space next to them.

The big man was like a jungle animal ready to respond to danger, and she realized that she always thought of this man in terms of lean, sinewy, dangerous animal instinct and awareness. The attraction that crackled between them was inescapable, and for the first time she knew that she wanted this man on the most primitive level that existed between man and woman, a realization that for some reason surprised, shocked and strangely pleased her.

"Your friends?" he asked.

She recognized the car and the people in it. She nodded, turning back to him to find his eyes on her.

"Will we . . . see each other again?" she asked.

He lifted a hand, touching a finger to her cheek. An intimate gesture, not unlike a lover's. "Maybe we'll be smuggled out of Russia together. For now, lady, it's goodbye."

"For now," she emphasized. "And for always, Mack, thank you for changing my life in Afghanistan and for saving my life in Moscow. God protect you."

"And you," he replied. "Now go, Katrina. Live large."

"First, kiss me," she said, touching his fingers where they caressed her face. "Kiss me as if it were the last time."

He smiled at that. "You're shameless."

"Kiss me."

He kissed her, touching his lips to hers just long enough for the exquisite tenderness of it to join between them.

There was no more to say.

No more time.

She retained her grip on the blanket wrapped tightly around her prison uniform and let herself out of the car.

0730 HOURS.

Bolan felt human again.

He pushed the cleaned plate away from him, put down the silverware, leaned back in his chair at Tanya Yesilov's kitchen table and emitted a lengthy, heartfelt sigh of contentment. He looked at the breathtaking blonde across the table from him. She wore a snappy tweed skirt and jacket ensemble that made her look like a model out of a high-fashion magazine.

"Thanks, Tanya. I needed that. The inner man has been satisfied."

He had driven directly to Tanya's after parting with Katrina but had not parked the Volvo in its designated parking space behind her building where he'd found it.

Groholski Street, where this lovely CIA "sleeper" maintained her living quarters, was a quiet residential street an hour since emptied of most respectable working Muscovites. He could not afford to take chances after what had gone down less than an hour before across town, after his bustout of Katrina from Lefortovo.

He had parked the Volvo a block away and had approached Tanya's apartment building from the opposite direction, feeling conspicuous walking down the snowy sidewalk, passing only an occasional woman with children on her way to market, a postman, a smattering of delivery men, but no one else.

He had reconnoitered the block as best he could without appearing to be idle, discerning no enemy presence, no men sitting in any of the cars parked along the curb, no one appearing to loiter about more than they should, as if on the lookout for him.

He had hurried along on foot through the back alley, letting himself in through the rear entrance of the building with one of the keys on the chain that Tanya had lent him to use her car.

He had carefully made his way up to her flat, and she had appeared very happy to see him. But she had not expressed this with the same physical contact as when he had been on his way from there to rescue Katrina.

Bolan thought again of the disparities between the cool sensuality of Tanya and the exuberant energy of Katrina and how he felt himself somehow drawn to them both.

Tanya cleared away the dishes from before him.

She had prepared a simple, delicious breakfast of bacon, eggs, toast and plenty of black coffee. Finished the meal, Bolan helped himself to another cup of coffee from the pot on the table.

Tanya crossed to the sink to rinse off the dishes with all the efficiency of a housewife about to send hubby and the seven kids off about their day's business. She turned when she had finished rinsing the dishes and looked at him across the table from where she stood, her back to the sink.

"It is a thirty-minute drive from here to Balashika. We should leave now."

He did not need to be told, but he had needed the brief respite from activity the past half hour had provided. He had not allowed himself to slow down since the dissident group, which had smuggled him to Moscow from the border, had left him to rendezvous with Katrina and her two unfortunate friends, Andrei and Vladimir.

He felt human again, yes, no small thanks to Tanya's hospitality and her womanly touch in the kitchen, reminding Bolan of the role she had played for her KGB bosses when he and Tanya had first encountered each other in Iran.

At that time the blonde had initially pretended to be Ellie Talbot, sassy American housewife stranded by circumstances in Teheran. He had learned something about her when they had taken fire together in Iran, and now he realized anew, with her cooking digesting comfortably in his stomach, what a tantalizing enigma the woman was.

She had touched his soul in Iran at a point in his life when he had started to think the loss of April, the loss of all those loved ones victimized along his bloody miles, had perhaps robbed him of that essential element in a normal man's makeup—*feeling*.

He and this CIA spy who called herself Tanya had been through a lot in a very short time in Teheran. And in Moscow, for that matter. He owed her.

It wasn't a flagging spirit that the scrubdown he had administered himself in her bathroom had revived—he didn't need that—but it had eased the muscular aches and it had recharged him.

He had not showered—the latex mask would not permit it—and Bolan had no wish to be caught naked in this city, this close to the showdown with archenemy Greb Strakhov.

There were many questions crowding his subconscious, and they now came into sharper focus. He found himself not sure what to think of the lovely across the table from him.

"It might be a good idea for you to sit this one out, Tanya," he said, setting down his empty coffee cup.

"The trip to the Group *Nord* meeting, I mean. 'Sergei Fedorin' has enough authority to get in on his own."

She straightened, her beauty masked by surprise, concern. "Sit it out?" She repeated the colloquialism in Russian, the language they spoke to each other. "But my presence in Balashika is intended to furnish you with close-in support."

"It's your decision to make," he conceded. "There's going to be a lot of killing on that base within the next hour."

"I understand, of course."

"There'll be bullets flying. I wouldn't want you to catch one."

"My orders are to go to that complex with you," she responded adamantly. "You know what I can do—my capabilities. Why do you say these things to me?"

"This is the time to take out the KGB bosses," he reminded her. "Their power politics are a mess. The timing for a hit like this couldn't be better. You and your CIA bunch stand to gain plenty if I pull this one off."

She eyed him without blinking. "All the more reason for me to be along. There is something else, is it not so?"

"There's plenty. There's that flare gun of Strakhov's, the one Petrovsky told us about."

"What can that have to do with anything?"

"I don't know. That's just it. That flare gun is just another wrinkle in the fabric. A question without an answer, and it could mean a lot. I don't like questions without answers."

"There has to be more," she insisted. "You are not telling me everything, Mack."

"I'm telling you what I want to tell you. Your cover for the Company will be crucially jeopardized by what's about to happen at Balashika if it doesn't go down right."

"Would my position, my work, not be far more jeopardized were I not to put in my scheduled appearance at the Group *Nord* briefing? My regular job is to transcribe the minutes of the meeting. It's a chance I shall have to take, going there with you, and in any event, judging by what you accomplished at Lefortovo, I must say I feel safer at your side than I would anywhere else in Moscow!"

"What do you know about what happened at Lefortovo?" he asked quietly. "It hasn't made the radio or television news, has it?"

"Of course not, darling. This is Russia, remember? It never will 'make the news' as in America."

"Then how do you know what happened there?"

Her anger flared, her eye contact with him a glare. "You are serious, are you not?"

"Always. I ran into beefed-up security at the prison. They didn't increase the guard around the whole place, just around the building where Katrina was being held. As if they expected me."

"Are you implying that I told them?"

"Tell me you didn't."

She crossed the kitchen and came to where he rose from his chair. She stood less than six inches from him, looking squarely into his eyes.

"I am on your side, Mack. You can believe that or not, but it is true."

"Then we'll say no more about it."

"Perhaps you have fought alone for too long," she said.

She took hold of his right hand between both of her hands. She raised his arm and placed the palm of his hand on her chest above the heart, so that he could feel her heartbeat while the edge of his hand could feel the rise of her firm left breast beneath her clothing.

"Tanya—"

"Have you forgotten that others know in their hearts the same determination and devotion to duty that drives you? There are others in this world, Mack, trying to do something about it. I am one of them. Do not let what you go through blind you to this. Too much sacrifice can make a stone of the heart."

He withdrew his hand. "I expected a lot of things on this mission," he told her. "Having Yeats quoted to me by a beautiful spy wasn't one of them."

She smiled at his recognition of the quote. "You see, Executioner, we are two of a kind. I will not stay behind when you leave to take on the enemy. I would have thought you knew this about me, if nothing else."

"Maybe I just had to be sure. Okay, Tanya, you're in. Let's do it."

"Let me get my coat."

A minute later she rejoined Bolan in the kitchen where she picked up her purse and followed him to the doorway of the apartment. He motioned her to step aside, unleathering the Beretta from its shoulder rig with his right hand, his left reaching for the door handle. He stood on the opposite side of Tanya across the doorway.

She read the caution in his eyes and unsnapped her purse, reaching inside to withdraw a Walther PPK. It remained concealed from casual view of anyone passing by in the hallway as Bolan opened the door, but he saw her index finger curved around the Walther's trigger just in case.

He held his Beretta ready but out of sight against the wall, holding his position for a moment before filling the doorway. He motioned Tanya to stay with him, peered up and down the corridor and, seeing no one, holstered the Beretta and motioned her on through.

They scurried down to the stairway at the far end of the corridor, descending to the back alley entrance, retracing Bolan's approach to the building of an hour earlier. They made it to the Volvo without encountering or detecting any surveillance of the apartment building or of the neighborhood. When they reached the Volvo, Bolan took the steering wheel and they drove away.

Little had changed during his brief R & R spent in the apartment of Tanya Yesilov. Sunshine had turned the snow to dirty slush. This, too, being plowed and scooped by the city's efficient street crews. Traffic had thinned some, the morning rush hour over earlier than it would have been in any American city.

Bolan had a pretty good idea of Moscow's layout. He navigated the Volvo onto Bolshaya Kaluzhskaya Street, south of the river, and drove east past the Presidium of the USSR Academy of Science.

The boulevards and secondary streets were no longer clogged with office workers scurrying to their jobs; now it hummed with the general hubbub of any large city. There were students and citizens enjoying their time off, and a few tourists moved about gawking at the city, but notably lacking were any signs of the destitute, the poverty stricken, the "street people" one would see in an American city and not, Bolan knew, because such problems did not exist in the Soviet Union.

Far from it.

Since Khrushchev's time Soviet leaders had been staking their legitimacy on promises to raise the standard of living. But endless shortages of consumer goods and housing, not to mention a decaying health care system, had brought about a severe loss of public faith and a decline in "civic morale." This state of affairs gave rise, Bolan was well aware, to statistics of rising corruption, crime and alcoholism, the latter being prevalent throughout Soviet society.

The streets of Moscow are clean of "street people," because anyone unemployed is considered a parasite of the state and sent to the work camps, so that the nation's capital can be held out to the West as a showplace glowing with the success of the Soviet system.

Before long the mishmash of sleek, modern and cuppolaed historical architecture gave way to suburban sprawl, which eventually yielded to open countryside. Bolan navigated the Volvo on course toward the Balashika complex fifteen kilometers east of the Moscow city limits.

No conversation passed between Bolan and Tanya during the drive, as if by mutual consent each desired to be alone with their thoughts this close to tackling the mission objective.

It was almost impossible for even Bolan to believe that it had been less than twenty-four hours since Hal Brognola had apprised him of the situation inside the KGB, of the scheme suggested through CIA channels by the woman who now sat beside him.

"Anton Petrovsky" was in place, and as Brognola had explained to Bolan, and which Bolan had told Tanya, the timing could not be better to mount this command strike at the hierarchy, the bosses, the *nachalstvo*, of the KGB.

It had brought Bolan back to Stony Man Farm and the grave, the memory, of April Rose. Then the flight to Helsinki and the dissident underground railway into the USSR. To Moscow, where just about everything about this mission started going to hell except for the rescue of Katrina.

Bolan took satisfaction in that, but it did not take away the sadness when he thought of the fate of two dissidents named Vladimir and Andrei, of Niktov, and most especially of a large-living woman named Zara who lived no more.

The objective lay dead ahead.

As did, maybe, answers to those questions without answers, like a flare gun that could mean anything and the enigma of a beautiful blonde named Tanya.

The only thing on his side was the fact that he was Sergei Fedorin of the Sixteenth Directorate, and the life mask he wore would prevent witnesses at Lefortovo from identifying Mack Bolan as the attacker who had freed Katrina.

And there was comfort in knowing that after this hit, if he survived, he was set up to be whisked out of Russia immediately upon his withdrawal from the KGB complex.

He steered the Volvo to within half a kilometer of the KGB complex, closing the distance across forest-bordered, lightly traveled secondary roads.

This was it.

Strakhov.

The KGB high command.

The mission.

This one's for you, April.

13

"Excuse me, but could either of you gentlemen spare a cigarette?" the President of the United States asked.

The two Secret Service men had maintained a discreet visible shadow of the Man while he had strolled deep in thought for the preceding thirty minutes.

The agents—the President knew their names: Jim Brewster and Larry Togota, men whose orders included laying down their lives for the safety of the Chief Executive if necessary—reacted with startled expressions from alert young faces that would not have blinked at anything, including weapons spitting death.

"Sir?" Brewster asked blankly.

The President had earned a well-known reputation as a militantly reformed ex-smoker.

Togota produced a pack of cigarettes from his jacket pocket, extending them.

"There you are, sir."

"Thanks, Larry."

He took a cigarette and a light, proffered by the bodyguard of Japanese descent, then turned from them to continue his seemingly aimless stroll, thinking about Bolan and what he, the President of these United States, should do about the Executioner.

The early-evening air carried a nip that contrasted with the warmth of the preceding spring day. Traffic sounds carried from Pennsylvania Avenue, but except for that a sense of seclusion permeated the heavily foliaged walkways through and near the Rose Garden.

He took two puffs of the cigarette and felt distaste pull his facial muscles at the unpleasant bite of tobacco irritating his throat, lungs and sinuses.

He extinguished the cigarette with the heel of his shoe and pocketed the butt for later disposal, wondering how he could ever have enjoyed the foul things for thirty years.

He also wondered why the human, one-on-one problems that came his way were always the ones to cause him to lose more sleep, get more upset stomachs, take the longest time to mentally wrestle with.

Like the Bolan problem.

Oh, he worried plenty about the state of this sad old world, he reminded himself.

There were the arms race, the Middle East, Latin America; every day brought new lines to the once distinguished campaign poster visage, giving the President a far more haggard appearance than he cared to admit.

He had the best minds in the country, in the western world, sharing the burden of those problems, though, aiding him with their collective expertise.

The one-on-ones could only be grappled with in the torment of his private soul.

Like the Bolan problem.

He had inherited Stony Man Farm and the Executioner from a previous administration, yet there was scant precedent for dealing with a man like Bolan because, quite simply, in this President's estimation, despite past differences there never had been a man like Bolan.

The Executioner was one of a kind and so was his loyalty to a government that had done nothing but complicate what the modern warrior was trying to do with skills, values and a sense of honor.

The President made his decision.

He turned to the executive mansion, the Secret Service men maintaining their distance, allowing the Man the privacy of his thoughts.

Brewster and Togota followed him into the White House. They drew up, taking their posts in the corridor outside the office.

The Man strode behind his desk, took a seat and reached for his telephone. He punched the button to connect him with the central scrambler.

"Blue Foxtrot Delta," he said to the computer at the other end.

He sat hunched over his desk, waiting for the connection to be made.

Hoping he was not too late.

BROGNOLA HUNG UP THE PHONE with the President's words ringing in his ears. He turned in his swivel chair to Bear Kurtzman, who sat in a wheelchair next to him at the main console of the Stony Man Farm computer room.

They had spent the day in near-silent vigil, by unspoken mutual consent, waiting on some word out of Russia on the progress of Bolan's mission.

There had been no word.

Activity had subsided in and out of the computer room and the underground complex surrounding it. Farm personnel were on twenty-four-hour alert during crisis situations, but at this moment Phoenix Force was on their way to a job and would be in transit for the next seven hours. Able Team was on its way in from a particularly difficult mission in the Andes.

The Bolan situation was classified above standard Stony Man personnel access, except for Brognola and Kurtzman, and even they had not been given the whole picture.

Brognola patted his pockets for matches to light the cold stogie that he had been chewing on for the past hour. Finding no matches, he just kept chewing. His stomach felt like butterflies were having an air war inside it.

Kurtzman looked up from the display screen. "Bingo. Just heard from the Moscow cell that got Striker in. Limited communication, of course. Our man is in, arrangements to get him out within the hour are on standby, and if I read between what few lines there are, there's some sort of hell to pay that has nothing to do with the mission objective." Bear nodded to the phone in front of Hal. "Anything?"

"The Man has made his decision. He's backing our guy, told the CIA boss to go screw himself, or diplomatic words to that effect."

Kurtzman studied his friend. "So why the gloom? Striker's got his backup the way he's supposed to have. It's going down the way we want it to, right?"

"It hasn't gone down yet," Brognola reminded him. "We have the Company out of our hair, but I still don't like it. The President called Striker a 'magnificent anachronism.' He said it like he was delivering a goddamn eulogy."

"I know what's eating you, Hal. You wish it was you and the big guy back on the streets again, don't you? Where a man knew he was backed up by the best, that others would stand behind him. You wish it was that way instead of you sitting here and our man inside Russia."

"Maybe it'll be that way again," Brognola grumbled. "But right now I want that dude back in one piece."

"He'll make it," Bear said. "So long as the Company doesn't foul things up, the big guy will pull this one off no matter how tough it is."

Brognola removed what was left of the cigar from his mouth and threw it in the vicinity of the nearest wastebasket. "I hope the hell you're right, Bear. We're down to the finish line. That's when something always goes wrong."

GREB STRAKHOV SAT AT HIS DESK, his back warmed by the sunlight streaming through his window from the snow across busy Dzerzhinsky Square.

He ignored the full cup of tea in front of him, concentrating instead on the saucer of lemon wedges next to the cup, sucking on the wedges one after the other, allowing the tart bite to awaken his senses, something the stopover and shower at his apartment on Petushka Street had been unable to accomplish.

There was so much to consider, especially in light of what had happened at Lefortovo Prison two hours ago. He wondered what would happen within the next half hour when he and Bolan faced each other across the width of a room. Who would live, who would die? There could be no way of knowing, of course. He had never underestimated the big American warrior, and he did not intend to start now.

He set aside the teacup and the saucer, which was now filled with lemon wedge rinds. He withdrew his pistol and double-checked the load and action.

The intercom phone on his desk buzzed. He holstered the pistol and answered the phone. His secretary in the outer office told him, "Major Petrovsky to see you, sir."

"Very good. Send him in."

He set down the phone receiver, leaned back in his chair and waited. The office door opened and Petrovsky stepped in. There were dark circles under his eyes. He carried a folded and sealed dispatch. He saluted sharply.

"Good morning, Major General."

Strakhov did not return the salute, as was his custom. He nodded to the dispatch. "What have you there?"

Petrovsky set the piece of paper on the desk. "For Your Eyes Only, sir. Comm section asked me to walk it over on my way through. It just came in. And I have our automobile waiting for the drive to Balashika."

"You have heard what happened at Sokolniki Park last night?"

"Yes, sir. I received word just as I was seeing to your orders to increase security checkpoints around the city.

It appears our additional precautions were, uh, a bit late.''

"So it does. And have you received word of the activities at Lefortovo Prison?''

Petrovsky shifted his weight—uncomfortably, Strakhov thought—where he stood facing the major general's desk.

"I am . . . afraid that is news to me, sir. I have been busy collating the necessary reports and data for the Group *Nord* meeting, as I understood you wanted done. Is . . . something wrong?''

Strakhov picked up the folded paper, motioning Petrovsky to the stiff-backed chair facing his desk. "Not at all, Major, not at all. Do have a seat. Forgive my brusque manner. Morning is never my best time, as you will learn. Let me see what this is before we leave.''

"As you wish, sir. Thank you.''

"Help yourself to the tea.'' Strakhov indicated the pot with a nod as he broke the seal on the message.

"Thank you, Major General. I believe I will,'' Petrovsky said, leaning forward to pour himself a cup.

Strakhov read, mentally decoding the message with a practiced ease that was second nature to him. He read the missive twice, then set it down on his desk, experiencing a glow of satisfaction.

"Is it something regarding the man Bolan, sir?''

"As a matter of fact, it is, Major, and it is ironic you should be here with me when I received it. There are some things you should know before we leave for Balashika.''

"Sir?''

Strakhov leaned back in his chair, regarding the man sitting across from him. "You are aware of our recent progress in gaining access to the computerized scrambler of the American intelligence system?"

"I am."

"We have intercepted a most interesting telephone conversation between the President of the United States and a gentleman named Harold Brognola. You do recognize that name."

"From the Executioner file, yes, sir."

"Very good. A trap is about to be sprung, Major, as I told you this morning. Would you like to hear more about it?"

"But of course, Major General."

Strakhov pointed to the piece of paper Petrovsky had brought him. "That is a transcript of the conversation between the President of the United States and Brognola. The President has informed Brognola that the CIA will support Mack Bolan during his present mission into Moscow as will a local cell of dissidents. There had been some doubt, you see, as to whether or not the CIA would provide support, considering their cross-purposes with the Executioner."

"I thought the Americans had detected our tapping into the Blue Foxtrot Delta system."

Strakhov rose from the desk, turning away from Petrovsky, clasping his hands behind his back to stare out at the square without really seeing anything down there.

"It is a fact they did discover our entry tap, yes. It was the first glimmer we had that they had a man planted high in our organization. At the very top."

A pause.

"Any idea who the spy is, sir?"

"I devised a plan, with some help," Strakhov said, staring vacantly at the window before him. "The fact that we were able to reenter Blue Foxtrot Delta's computers after their programs had been changed really has little bearing on what I am about to tell you. I mention it only because that communication you brought me serves as proof positive that my plan is about to reach fruition, Major. And you are to play an important part in the final act."

"I had hoped to, Major General. I am at your disposal."

"Yes, I know." Strakhov turned, picked up the remaining unsucked lemon wedge from the dish on his desk. He sucked at it, nodding to Petrovsky's empty teacup. "Please do help yourself to another, Major."

"Thank you, sir."

Petrovsky appeared perfectly at ease. Unsuspecting. Good, thought Strakhov.

"The telephone conversation between the President and Brognola indicates that in the mission they have sent Bolan on, their objective is about to be achieved or, I should say, attempted."

"The objective most certainly being you, sir," Petrovsky said. "Us, that is to say, as you surmised."

"Indeed, I am the Executioner's objective," Strakhov said, nodding. "As he is mine."

He left the desk to move idly about his office as he spoke, strolling over to absently restraighten a marble bust of Lenin atop a filing cabinet.

"It was Bolan in Sokolniki Park then?" Petrovsky asked. "And at Lefortovo?"

Strakhov nodded. "And you need not trouble yourself too much about not having tightened security around the city in time to stop him." He moved to glance over a shelf of manuals behind the executive officer. "You see, Bolan coming to Moscow was my idea."

Petrovsky half turned in his chair, craning a surprised look at his superior. "Your idea, sir? The trap you mentioned?"

"You catch on quickly. I will admit the events at the prison were not anticipated by me, but I should have suspected it. Damn me for an old fool. I have been outfoxed too many times by that wily American, but he is walking into *my* trap now and nothing will save him."

"Balashika?"

Strakhov nodded, eyeing Petrovsky closely. "Balashika. You see, Major, *I* have been guiding Bolan to his death, not his superiors, not Fate, but *I*, Greb Strakhov."

He curbed himself when he heard the rising passion of his own voice.

Petrovsky uncomfortably shifted his attention away from the major general, returning to set his teacup on Strakhov's desk, his back to where the major general stood at the shelf of manuals and regulations.

"I see . . ." Petrovsky seemed to be speaking more to himself than to Strakhov. "It *was* Bolan then."

Strakhov stepped away from the shelf, loosening his tie. "What is that, Major?"

"Er, at the prison, I mean," Petrovsky said a bit more brightly. "I mean, there isn't any doubt it was Bolan then, is there, sir?"

Strakhov remained standing behind Petrovsky. The KGB chief began to undo his necktie.

"I made a slight, intended error of speech a few moments ago, Major. I said I had a few things to discuss with you before we left for the Group *Nord* meeting. In fact, *we* will not be leaving."

He pulled his tie from around his neck, grasping one end in each fist.

Petrovsky started to turn.

"What do you—" he began, managing to turn halfway around.

"*I* will attend the meeting and *I* will see Mack Bolan die," Strakhov spat in a ferocious whisper, taking a quick step forward to stand directly behind Petrovsky. "You, my dear Major, will be dead. You were the bait, along with myself, and you are no longer needed."

He looped the necktie around Petrovsky's throat before the executive officer could fully turn in the chair or stand.

Strakhov yanked both ends of the tie together behind his victim's neck, twisting the tie, tugging both ends outward.

Petrovsky sat bolt upright, raising his hands frantically to claw at the material of the necktie digging into his throat, cutting off his wind.

Strakhov felt himself smile as he relentlessly applied more pressure.

Petrovsky almost managed to stand and turn, but his breathing was ragged now, his face flushing red, his eyes popping as if they would burst from their sockets, and he did not have enough strength to resist.

Strakhov slammed him back into the chair, then loosened the strangling necktie, not enough to allow the man in the chair to fully breathe, but enough to grant Petrovsky a few more seconds of life to hear what he had to say.

"I have known about you for weeks, Major, whatever your real name is. I have known you were CIA. I knew they wanted you where I am or close to it and, yes, you were the bait. You were not a very good executive officer, and you were a worse spy. You are not at my disposal, dear Major. You are disposed of. Give my regards to Bolan when you meet him in hell."

Strakhov jerked on the necktie, once more tightening it around his victim's throat, twisting, pulling each end of the tie in opposite directions with all his might, forcing Petrovsky's squirming, wildly spastic body against the back of the chair.

Petrovsky's grip slackened from Strakhov's arms. The major's struggling ceased, and all that remained then were small body twitches and the staccato drumming of the dying man's heels on the office floor. Then the hands dropped to his side, the feet stopped beating and Petrovsky's body went limp.

Strakhov continued twisting and pulling the ends of the necktie for another full minute, then he loosened his grip and let one end of the tie drop. He watched the corpse sag to the floor like a man curling up to sleep except that Petrovsky's face had a bright purple hue and his tongue stuck out of his mouth like a rotting sausage. And then the body emitted a wet, flatulent sound of escaping gas.

Strakhov stared down at his handiwork for several seconds, the tie dangling forgotten from one hand. He was out of breath, his heart pounding.

I've been behind a desk for too long, he realized. He had forgotten the sensation of taking a human life, of ending another's existence slowly so the victim knew what was happening, that their world was ending and there was nothing to save them. . . .

He reminded himself that this was but the overture, the prelude of the trap about to be sprung precisely as he had envisioned it from the very start.

He glanced at his watch.

0750.

Good. He would be several minutes late for the Group *Nord* meeting.

That would give Bolan something to think about.

There would be time enough for the sensations Strakhov felt stirring within himself now—strange, exciting, forbidden sensations when he remembered the death struggle of the man he had just slain.

He had been a stranger to sensation for too long, he decided, with only the cold hatred for Bolan ruling his life. He had been governing his private empire within the KGB almost as if by rote, but sensation was returning now, and after Bolan there would be time, yes, to spend the money, to disappear, a new identity, a life of riches and forbidden sensation.

He felt more alive than he had in years.

He pocketed his watch and stepped around Petrovsky's corpse to the phone, dialing as he stood regarding the dead body of the man the CIA thought they could plant without the head of the Thirteenth Section finding out about it.

"Come to my office," Strakhov ordered curtly when a connection was made. "I will not be here. There is garbage on the floor. See that it is removed."

He did not wait for a reply. He hung up the telephone and left his office, heading for the car Petrovsky had arranged to take them to Balashika.

The moment of truth was at hand.

14

Bolan slowed, steering the Volvo off the stretch of blacktop that led into dense forest alongside the highway before curving out of sight.

"We are almost there," Tanya said quietly. Ominously, he thought.

He drove at a reduced speed along blacktop wet from snow that melted beneath a bright sun climbing into a clear sky of cobalt blue. It would be another warm spring day. Traces of the snowstorm would be gone by noon or before.

He wondered if he would be alive to see that.

Spring had always been his favorite time, even as a kid back home in Massachusetts. Spring, a time of birth, rebirth and hope.

Bare trees overhead hemmed in either side of the blacktop for half a kilometer before a clearing of about 250 square meters spread out before them.

A sentry wearing the khaki uniform of the militia stood just before a chain link fence gate on which a sign read: Scientific Research Center. The militiaman pointed an AK-47 directly at the Volvo, finger on the trigger, holding his left arm up and out in a stern halt gesture.

A guard shack stood inside and to the right of the entrance to the research center. It was the only entrance, Bolan discerned with a quick eyeball of the perimeter.

He braked the Volvo to a stop.

He saw at least a dozen militiamen posted around the outside and inside of the closed gate, and not one of these sentries looked the least bit relaxed or slack in their duties; every eye, every gun barrel was aimed at the car and its two occupants.

The sentry before the gate strode to Bolan's side of the vehicle, not removing his finger from the AK's trigger.

"These are KGB dressed as militia," Tanya whispered to Bolan without moving her lips. "They will miss nothing."

The sentry stopped next to Bolan's open window.

"Identification!" the guard barked.

Tanya reached into her purse and handed across what Bolan knew to be her special pass, required by anyone hoping to gain entrance into this most highly classified of all KGB bases. She gave the sentry a buff-colored plastic card with her photo and a perforated code designating the areas in which Agent Yesilov had authorization to enter. The sentry studied the photo, looked back at the blonde beside Bolan and handed the card back.

Bolan showed the sentry his ID, the one furnished by Niktov.

This got a reaction.

The sentry blinked a couple of times and all of a sudden appeared very eager to hand the card back to "Sergei Fedorin." He stepped back from the car and ordered the men inside to open the gate and let the vehicle pass.

There was one exception to gaining entrance into the Balashika Base without the special pass, and Bolan had it.

No one wanted to cross a man from the Sixteenth Directorate.

He slipped the Volvo into gear and rolled forward into the base, taking in as much as possible during the drive up the four-hundred-meter incline to a nearly filled parking lot.

The high chain link fence, topped with barbed wire, ran the full unbroken perimeter of the base. He spotted walking three-men patrols all the way around.

A helicopter landing pad, alongside the parking lot, hosted three Mi-24 Hinds, the same type of gunship that had closed in on Bolan and Katrina Mozzhechkov's group when Bolan had first arrived in the Moscow vicinity. He knew these gunships were obviously on standby for defensive purposes in case of an attack.

"Sergei Fedorin," attaché case in hand, and Tanya Yesilov, stylish in her tan belted raincoat, left the Volvo and walked to the seven-story structure adjacent to the parking lot on the far side, a modern building of aluminum and glass shaped like a three-pointed star.

The objective.

Headshed of the State Committee for Security.

Not Dzerzhinsky Square, but right here for the one day of the month when the Group *Nord* meeting was held with the top echelon of every KGB operational division present and accounted for.

The First Chief Directorate Building.

The high command.

Bolan felt every fiber of his being attuned to the vibrations and dangers of this place.

He held the front double glass door open for Tanya and followed her into the marble foyer. They again had to pause to show their IDs to sentries standing just inside the main entrance. And again the sentries carefully checked Tanya against the photo of her pass. And again the sentries treated "Sergei Fedorin" with all the respect and efficiency of men coming into contact with a carrier of some fatal disease.

Tanya and "the man from the Sixteenth Directorate" strode on past the newsstand and cafeteria to a bank of elevators. Bolan noticed that he drew scant attention except from those sentries who knew who he was, or thought they did.

The lobby of the headquarters building buzzed with human activity, mostly men in uniform, their attention on the svelte figure of the blonde in the trench coat that clung to healthy long legs and a classy chassis as she and Bolan strode to the elevators.

This was the way Bolan wanted it.

She pressed the button, and in the moment it took for the car to arrive he did a careful pan around the lobby without pretending to do so, spotting and placing armed men in uniform for future reference.

The elevator doors whispered open, and he and Tanya stepped inside. They had the car to themselves. She again pushed the button they wanted to the third floor, and the elevator started up.

They glanced at each other. She started to speak, but Bolan shook his head. It was barely perceptible, but she saw it and understood what he was telling her. No conversation. There could be, probably were, microphones and cameras every couple of feet in a place like this, and they would not miss the elevators.

She acknowledged with a flicker of her lovely green eyes, and they looked straight ahead during the brief time before the doors hissed open again.

They stepped out into a marble corridor where a cluster of some thirty men stood amid an atmosphere of more or less friendly idle chatter and drifting clouds of cigarette smoke; the heads of various KGB operational divisions engaging in conversation with one another were easy to spot from the equal number of tight-lipped, slit-eyed bodyguards who hovered near their respective bosses.

One man saw Bolan and Tanya emerge from the elevator and came toward them, a stout fellow of about five foot eight, a cheery smile pasted across his cherubic face.

"Ah, Tanya, my dear, how nice to see you. You look ravishing as ever. And who is your friend?" he inquired with a good-natured, though professional, appraisal of Bolan.

Bolan recognized him.

Viktor Frolov, in charge of Directorate S, the unit that illegally infiltrates disguised KGB officers into other nations.

"My name is of no consequence," Bolan bluntly snarled at one of the most powerful men in the KGB. He showed Frolov his Sixteenth Directorate ID. "Why are you men not in the conference room?"

Frolov turned several shades paler when he realized who he was addressing. "Why, we were . . . we are waiting for Major General Strakhov. He seems to be a few minutes late.''

Bolan caught the glance Tanya threw him.

A warning.

''I want everyone in the conference room,'' the man disguised as Sergei Fedorin ordered. ''Immediately.''

''The bodyguards?'' Frolov asked.

Bolan shook his head. ''In the hallway. Quickly now. I want everyone in place when Strakhov arrives.''

Frolov nodded uneasily and turned to rejoin the others.

Bolan and Tanya stood back as the party in the hallway began breaking up, Frolov whispering Bolan's instructions to the others.

Word got around fast. The bosses of the largest terror machine in history began docilely filing into the conference room at Bolan's command, though they and their bodyguards studied him with long, speculative looks that he returned with steely directness.

He recognized this bunch, to a man.

Savages all.

These were the ones who pulled the strings. The ones who caused the suffering in Afghanistan, in Poland, throughout the Third World, and even in their own homeland, stifling freedoms and growing fat on loot extracted from the decent of the world who had too much decency to fight back.

These were the cannibals, those of the species driven by the dark side of human nature, who feasted and grew obscenely from human suffering and grief.

The scum at the top and, yeah, Bolan had them mentally mug-filed to a man.

He spotted Albert Kulagin, slim and dapper in a French-cut suit. Boss of the Twelfth Department of senior officers who, having proven themselves abroad, had been given carte blanche to chase and capture any quarry anywhere in the world.

Oleg Liyepa, as swarthy and simian-looking as the photos Bolan had seen of him. Chief of the Fifth Directorate, the dirtiest part of the KGB; the crud entrusted with prosecuting religious opposition and silencing all elements of dissidence.

Aleksei Obinin, head of the Technical Operations Directorate, which developed new poisons, weapons and the like; the directorate responsible, in fact, for developing the attaché case acquired by Bolan from Niktov.

Obinin gave no indication that he recognized anything familiar about ''Sergei Fedorin's'' attaché case, if he saw it at all and, after all, one of its primary benefits was that the case carried by Agent ''Fedorin'' looked no different from any other; there were at least a dozen black attaché cases in the crowded hallway.

Last but not least, among the fifteen men filing into the conference room, Bolan identified middle-aged Yevgenni Trekhlebov, pleasant-looking in a family-man sort of way; the guy responsible for overseeing Active Measures, which is propaganda, disinformation, sabotage, terrorism and murder committed for psychological effect.

Trekhlebov worked closely with any number of international terrorist groups, bombings, arson and killings by terrorists essential in buttressing Active Measures campaigns by generating social unrest, creating the illusion, the impression, that a society may be degenerating into chaos.

These men and the eleven with them were the ones Bolan had come to take out, counting on the Sixteenth Directorate ruse to pull him through. But that was not all he had counted on, and he noticed an essential element missing from the picture.

The bodyguards fell back along the walls of the hallway amid a murmuring of idle conversation, only a modicum of their attention directed at "Fedorin," who held slightly back from the others with Tanya.

Because the KGB is organized in a rigid, vertical chain of command, cronyism is widespread, particularly so at this level of the hierarchy. The KGB bosses continued chatting socially as they filed into the conference room, only a bit more subdued than before.

Bolan said to Tanya, speaking low enough so no one else could hear, "Petrovsky's not here."

"He should be. Perhaps he's coming with Strakhov."

"Yeah, perhaps. All right, let's join the party."

They crossed the hallway, moving past the bodyguards who eyed them without expression. Inside the conference room, fifteen bosses of the KGB were in the process of taking their seats at a long, polished oak conference table. A sideboard against one wall boasted carafes of water and cups.

Bolan knew there would be a bottle or three of vodka out of sight within easy reach in the cupboard below. It has been said that vodka is the water of Soviet life. The USSR has an extremely high rate of alcoholism, and this was nowhere as evident as in the ranks of these men, though they would stay clear of the bottle with a representative of the Sixteenth Directorate in their midst.

He closed the door behind them, spotting another door in the opposite wall of the long, airy room.

Tanya legged it directly over to a small separate desk against the wall, away from where the men sat at the conference table. She sat at the desk, uncovering a keyboard machine intended for keeping minutes of the meeting.

Bolan took a chair midway down the length of table facing the doorway at the nearest end of the room toward him. He could sense the tension increasing among those seated around the table, their conversation with one another decreasing to nothing, their attention turning to him.

He placed his attaché case on its side on the table before him.

Someone coughed nervously.

Viktor Frolov cleared his throat at one end of the table, opposite the vacant chair at the other end. "I, er, must apologize again, Agent Fedorin, for the major general's tardiness. I have, however, advised the rest of those of us present as to your identity."

"A most irregular procedure," Oleg Liyepa grumbled across the table from Bolan. "I should think those of us in the Group would have been advised of any sort of investigation directed our way by the Sixteenth Directorate."

Bolan eyed the guy coldly. "It is not your place to question, Comrade Liyepa, nor yours," he added to Frolov, "to apologize or patronize. I will tell you why I am here—"

He had no intention of starting this show until Strakhov put in an appearance. His role camouflage as a Sixteenth Directorate hit man had gotten him this far. He would have to ad lib now to maintain the illusion for just a few minutes more, he hoped.

He was interrupted as the door across from the hallway door, the one in the wall opposite near Bolan, opened. Greb Strakhov stepped in through that doorway from what looked like a narrow passageway of steps leading upward. Strakhov entered the room and closed the door after him. He turned to survey those seated around the table, "Sergei Fedorin" included.

Bolan felt a quickening of his pulse.

Frolov again cleared his throat with some visible discomfort. "Uh, Major General, this is Sergei Fedorin of the Sixteenth Directorate."

Bolan took the initiative before Strakhov could speak. "I understood Major Petrovsky would be present. Where is he?"

Strakhov remained where he stood near the door, eyeing "Fedorin" with something Bolan read as almost amusement where there should have been apprehension even from a man as high up in the organization as this boss of bosses.

"Petrovsky is dead, as you soon will be," Strakhov snarled at "Fedorin." "Uh-uh, keep your hands where we can see them . . . *Mack Bolan*. Gentlemen."

And the game suddenly went all to hell.

Every man seated at that table had positioned himself in such a way as to fast-draw a concealed weapon at this obviously prearranged signal. In the blink of an eye, every one of the KGB bosses had a pistol in his hand.

And fifteen gun barrels were aimed at Bolan before he could respond.

He obeyed Strakhov's command, keeping his hands on the attaché case on the table before him, one hand on either side. Bolan held eye contact with the man he had come so far to kill, but his peripheral vision panned the smug, amused faces of the men around the table and the guns trained on him.

He said to Strakhov in an almost conversational tone, "The whole charade, all the way back to me being brought in by Brognola, it was all a trap."

The KGB boss bowed slightly from the waist. "My sole regret, my dear Bolan, is that you wear that silly life mask, that I must see you die owning the features of another."

"Care to tell me how you worked it, or is that why I'm still breathing?"

A sneer crinkled the Russian's fleshy lips. "You retain your spirit right to the moment of your death. That is good. I admire you, Bolan. Under different circumstances, we could have been friends."

"Don't flatter yourself. I don't run with cannibals."

Strakhov lost the sneer. "I see. Very well, then, perhaps I have something that will shock you into losing your persistent arrogance."

Bolan remained looking straight ahead, but he could sense Tanya's presence behind him. His nostrils caught the faintest hint of perfume.

"I doubt it," he told Strakhov. Then, without turning, "Tanya, you lying, traitorous bitch."

The cool, round snout of the lady's Walther PPK touched lightly against the nape of his neck. "I'm sorry, lover," she told him in a low voice.

"Now you're the one flattering yourself. Why, Tanya? That's all I really want to know. Why did you change sides for real?"

She laughed, a mocking, soft tinkle of sound. "Why, they pay more, darling, of course. What other reason could there be?"

"None, I guess, for someone like you," he grated, almost spitting the words.

She chuckled, and the pistol retained its cool kiss against his flesh. "I must say, my big bad Executioner, you have hardly been at your best, either. I never thought I would get the drop on you this easily."

"Maybe it's just my way of making sure," he told her. Then he turned to Strakhov. "When Dragon Lady here sold out and told you about Petrovsky, you saw how you could nail two birds with one stone—the spy the CIA had planted next to you, and me."

"Two birds with one stone," Strakhov echoed with a mildly amused chuckle that did not sound pleasant at all. "You Americans have such a quaint way with your rather plain language. Yes, my dear enemy, that is exactly what I set out to do."

Bolan picked it up from there. "Coming from Tanya, the very agent they had planted to monitor Petrovsky, was enough to sell the Company, Brognola and the President."

Strakhov nodded, a wary gleam in his eye, tightening and loosening his hands into fists at his sides. "We lost you in Helsinki. Picked you up again when you arrived in Moscow, thanks to Agent Yesilov. It was Niktov who supplied you with your Sixteenth Directorate cover?''

"It's nice to know Niktov wasn't in on it," Bolan grunted. "I liked him."

"Dear no," Strakhov mused. "Citizen Niktov is one of the ones we were after, the swine, and all of the other cells of the dissident underground that assisted in your infiltration. They have all been targeted, thanks to you.

"The Mozzhechkov woman and her friends, the Gypsy scum who served Zara and Niktov... We have monitored you as much as possible. All over Moscow at this moment, and at several points between here and Helsinki, agents I have in place will close in when they are signaled that you are dead and it is over here."

"The flare gun," Bolan thought aloud.

Strakhov started visibly when he heard that.

"You know too much to live, Mack Bolan. This moment has been a long time in coming." Strakhov spat the words at Bolan. "You will never know the hours I have spent contemplating the sweetness of your death."

"I think maybe I would," Bolan growled, still as a statue before all the pistols pointing at him across the table. And he could feel the one the woman held against his neck. "I've spent the same amount of time waiting for this."

Strakhov considered that for an instant, Bolan could see. Then the cannibal chief, this evilest of the evil, April's killer, drew himself erect.

"Enough. The time has come to end it. I had anticipated pulling the trigger myself, but under the circumstances I think it would be far more enjoyable to those of us of the high council, as well as being a test of Agent

Yesilov's complete loyalty, were I to order the lady to blow your brains out. Are you quite agreeable to that, my darling?''

The barrel of the Walther PPK did not budge from the nape of Bolan's neck.

"I am," the blonde replied without inflection.

"Then kill him," Strakhov snarled. "I want to see the Executioner die."

Without saying another word, Tanya Yesilov squeezed the trigger.

Bolan's index fingers touched the panel buttons on either side of the attaché case in front of him—buttons not detectable by the naked eyes of those seated around the table. At the same instant he heard the metallic click instead of a gunshot from Tanya's Walther PPK.

Niktov had been killed back in Sokolniki Park before he could tell Bolan about the armament capabilities of the innocent-looking "attaché case," but Bolan knew all about this model of KGB spy equipment anyway. Two similar devices had been confiscated from the bodies of Russian agents from different points around the world, and the findings by CIA lab personnel had been issued to all Top Classified U.S. intelligence agencies, including Stony Man Farm.

Several things happened at once.

The fingering of the trigger mechanism of the "spy tool" fired off seven silenced rounds simultaneously from the front of the "attaché case," 9 mm bullets zapping several KGB bosses across from Bolan.

At the same instant, billowing clouds of poisonous white gas hissed, from concealed nozzles on either side of the attaché case, around the heads of those not struck by the bullets. Death spasms tightened trigger fingers as

the poison gas did its rapid, deadly work on Viktor Frolov, Aleksei Obinin and the rest.

As he triggered the firing mechanism of the attaché
case, Bolan dived sideways from his chair, still hearing
the click of the PPK Tanya had held against his neck.

He hit the carpeted floor of the conference room as
bullets fired by men already dead cut through the space
he had occupied a millisecond earlier.

He heard those bullets slap into Tanya Yesilov's body
before she had time to move or die from the poison gas
or figure out how he had managed a miracle.

Tanya, or whatever her real name was, died without
realizing Bolan had yielded to his gut suspicions and had
removed the bullets from her gun in her apartment during those moments when she had left him alone with her
purse in the kitchen while she had fetched her coat before the drive to Balashika.

The blonde toppled backward under the impact of the
projectiles as if yanked from her feet by a tremendous
tug of an invisible wire. The bullets wiped the beauty
from her face in a swirl of spurting blood and brains,
and other slugs dotted her high-fashion tweed ensemble, bullet holes spewing globs of red gore against the
wall behind her before she slammed into it, then pitched
forward unceremoniously in a crumpled heap.

Bolan looked away, unleathering his Beretta, the poison gas not affecting him because of specially designed
miniature nostril plugs that had also been in the attaché
case—the first clue for Bolan of what Niktov had given
him.

He peered up over the conference table, not ready to
believe Strakhov was dead until he saw it with his own

eyes, in time to see the door across from the hallway entrance slam shut behind running footsteps pounding up the stairway passage on the other side.

The cloud of poison gas dissipated, and fifteen deceased KGB savages, the best brains the enemy had in the espionage and world terror department, were nothing now but dead meat.

Strakhov had either been wearing the same type of nose plugs as Bolan—very possible, Bolan realized, considering how much Strakhov knew about the "Sergei Fedorin" deception—or the boss savage had been too fast for the gas to reach him. He had not been in range of bullets fired from the attaché case; there had probably been damn good reason why Strakhov had not left his standing position close to the door during the showdown.

Bolan darted toward the doorway through which Strakhov had disappeared.

The bodyguards in the hall made no effort to enter the room. Bolan had locked the door on his way in, confirming that this conference room would be ultrasound-proofed in addition to being free of bugging devices and the like. The top dogs of Group *Nord* would have had it no other way.

He charged around the end of the table to the doorway in pursuit of the real top dog, the evilest of the evil, hitting the door with a kick of rage and fury that punched it inward off its hinges. The Executioner leaped to the side, the Beretta in firing position, but no gunfire stabbed at him from the narrow stairway.

He heard the rapid footsteps of the Soviet spymaster's escape up beyond where the stairs curved around out of sight. Bolan dashed into the passageway without hesitation after the fleeing footfalls.

He had spent enough time hunting Strakhov down in their global cat-and-mouse dance of death to be able to read his enemy like a book. Strakhov was heading up to the roof to get his hands on the flare gun he must have secreted up there sometime before.

The boss savage had said it himself: the master plan called for more than simply terminating a CIA spy who had called himself Anton Petrovsky and an Executioner named Bolan.

Strakhov's plot also entailed the full-scale closing down of Moscow's already shaky dissident under-ground. Strakhov had men stationed all over Moscow, all over Russia; he had to know he could not trust any standard means of communication for something this big, with a CIA mole planted right in his own office. It had probably worried hell out of him when Petrovsky had walked in early that morning to see the major general receiving the flare pistol.

And it had come to this—Strakhov making his way to the roof to get his hands on the flare gun, to fire a col-ored flare into the sky above Moscow before Bolan could reach him. The flare would not only be a death sentence for untold Russian dissidents but would also summon reinforcements to the roof where Bolan would be trapped.

Bolan poured on the steam.

The stairway curved up and up, past closed doors, as Bolan gained on the escaping footfalls that sounded frantic now.

He heard a metal door bank open up there and knew Strakhov had made it to the roof.

And the flare pistol.

He burst through the doorway onto the flat roof of the building as Strakhov gained a low ledge fifty feet away and reached down under some bricks stacked there. Strakhov straightened, gripping the flare pistol. He whirled to see Bolan appear and tracked the flare pistol up, not at Bolan, but skyward.

Bolan leaped across the distance separating them, almost losing his balance on the slickness of melted snow coating the roof. A cruel grin of triumph curled Strakhov's fleshy lips when he saw Bolan lower the Beretta.

The Executioner charged forward.

Strakhov bent his finger around the trigger of the flare gun, his arm fully extending to fire the flare into the sky.

"You lose, Executioner."

Bolan did not fire the Beretta. He did not want a spastic death twitch from Strakhov to trigger the flare gun, sending a colored flare into the sky that would seal the fate of all those freedom fighters waging what good fight they could against the slave masters. He reached Strakhov before the KGB boss could pull the flare gun's trigger.

Strakhov's sneer turned into surprise and panic.

Bolan reached up to yank Strakhov's gun arm down, his grip on the Beretta making it difficult.

The Russian swung at Bolan, who started twisting Strakhov's arm once he had lowered it, forcing the flare gun around toward Strakhov's body.

Strakhov fought with every ounce of his strength to keep his aim from being turned in upon himself. He slipped his index finger away from the flare gun's trigger.

The two men's faces were inches apart, features distorted now with the effort of the struggle.

Then Strakhov realized what was about to happen, and his eyes widened in fear. He started to scream a plea at Bolan, but by this time Bolan already had the snout of the flare gun within two inches of Strakhov's abdominal region.

Bolan curved his own finger around the flare gun's trigger. He squeezed the trigger and released his hold of the flare gun, stepping back as he did so.

A thunderous roar blasted Strakhov away from Bolan, and his whole midsection appeared to explode from within.

A loud hissing sound almost drowned out the Russian's dreadful scream of agony as he backpedaled a couple of steps, the murderous hissing noise of white-hot magnesium buried deep in his intestines burning brightly.

The ledge of the roof stopped his backward progress, bending him back at the knees. Screaming his lungs out, clouded in the hissing stench of his own roasting flesh from the flare burning within his guts, Strakhov toppled, the screams following him all the way down. Then the cries ceased abruptly.

Bolan invested a few seconds in stepping forward to peer over the ledge. He saw Strakhov's body seven stories below, facedown, sizzling, melting snow that extinguished the live flare burning out his belly.

Bolan spared only a rapid look at the man he had come to kill, then he whirled, retracing his course back across the roof and into the raised shelter that led to the stairwell passage up which he had pursued Strakhov. He hustled down the stairs two at a time.

He had already seen, from the roof, immediate response to the grotesque sight of the red-colored, flare-enveloped body hurtling to its doom. He had glimpsed startled reactions from those who witnessed the fall, and at that moment he knew Strakhov's corpse would be surrounded by sentries and officers trying to make sense of what had happened.

A braying siren pierced the air from the complex outside the building as Bolan counted off the third floor on his way down, the stairs obviously reserved for the use of Strakhov and his top-echelon personnel.

The activity would be concentrated in the main hallways of the building, and if he did run into anyone he would either kill them or use the Sixteenth Directorate cover to exploit the confusion, whichever would seem handiest.

No one intercepted him on the stairs.

He reached the ground floor and the narrow doorway marking the end of Strakhov's secret stairway. He paused at the door, turning the handle with his free hand, and opened the door just enough to eyeball the scene outside separating him from the helicopter pad.

Three crewmen stood beside one of the choppers, which had been revved up to a low idle while Bolan had been busy inside the building. The crewmen, like almost everyone else he could see on the base, had their attention on the direction where Major General Strakhov had fallen.

He saw no one else across the yardage between the building and the landing pad with the three Hind gunships. Personnel scurried from different directions around the complex, the crowd growing in the less than sixty seconds since the man with the burning magnesium flare in his stomach had fallen from the roof. The flare's colored plumes of smoke rose no higher than the roof of the First Chief Directorate Building.

Bolan quit the stairwell doorway, advancing toward the chopper landing pad in the opposite direction as the personnel across the way running toward the bizarre occurrence at the other side of the building.

No one took notice of him.

In all the excitement throbbing through the research center at that moment, "Sergei Fedorin" could have been anyone racing to attend to some matter related to the KGB major general's fall.

He angled his rapid advance on the gunships in from the blind side of the crewmen. The first inkling they had that something was wrong was when the Executioner cut them down with withering auto fire from the silenced 93-R. Nine-millimeter zingers hosed the three crewmen into oblivion, their bodies flying to the ground, blocked from sight of all the activity as response to the occurrence near the building intensified.

For all Bolan knew, the bodyguards in the third-floor corridor may well have discovered the corpses of the other directorate bosses in the conference room by now, spreading the alert about that, too.

He jumped in through the side hatch door of the idling chopper and leaped toward the cockpit.

He revved the big bird to life, the rotor throb humming louder, drawing some attention from those around or rushing toward the headquarters building.

He worked the stick.

The helicopter rose from the pad.

He banked the chopper around, holding it in low hover.

He triggered two missiles that turned the other two gunships into mushrooming detonations of orange-red destruction.

That changed everything on the base, pulling every eye skyward.

Rifles, too.

Bolan piloted the gunship higher, banking her around again from a strafing run over the motor pool and parking lot.

He could hear bullets from below spanging off the Hind.

The chopper swept in fast and low, its rockets leaving twin paths of destruction below him, picking up vehicles left and right, demolishing the cars into unrecognizable hunks of smoldering metal, tearing human bodies as scattering KGB troopers were eaten up by the hammering, deafening concussions.

Bolan knew he had to get out of there on the double.

Planes, choppers and troops of every description would be receiving alert orders to deploy immediately to this base at this very instant; a hijacked Hind gunship would be easy enough to spot and shoot down before he could fly the Mi-24 more than a few klicks in any direction.

But he could not leave without a final farewell to the headshed of an enemy now without bosses to guide it because the Executioner had killed every one of them that mattered.

The Mi-24 was not taking hits, the fire down below too far out of range for them, but not for the ice-eyed man behind the chopper's controls.

He steadied the war bird and unleashed a couple of missiles at the seven-story structure that housed the First Chief Directorate.

It would be years before the terror network recovered from what the Executioner had wrought there today. He hovered around long enough to bear witness and feel good when missile after missile zeroed into different points of that modern temple of depravity; a fire burst here and another there the full length of the glass-and-aluminum structure, turning it into a raging inferno.

A funeral pyre for those trapped inside.

He pulled the chopper around for withdrawal, knowing he would have to set the Mi-24 down real fast.

They would have this area sectored off already, closing in.

He was not sure he would be able to make it.

Then he spotted the panel truck parked alongside the road, a half klick away from the base toward Moscow and the route he and Tanya Yesilov had driven here less than thirty minutes ago.

He lowered the chopper to treetop level and buzzed the truck. The three people who stood around it waved up at him.

He recognized the behemoth forms of Igor and Boris, the two black market undergrounders he had last seen bodyguarding Zara at the after-hours club in Moscow, before he had met Niktov.

Katrina Mozzhechkov stood between the Gypsy giants, waving with both arms at the chopper and sending worried looks down the road in the direction of the base. But Bolan saw no traffic in sight yet, military or civilian, except for the parked truck.

He set the chopper down behind a stretch of trees where the gunship could be easily spotted from the air but not from ground forces if they arrived first.

He left the armored pilot seat of the Hind, debarking at a run while the rotors were still whirling.

He jogged toward the truck and the trio around it. He grabbed the top of the latex mask at the base of the neck and yanked it from his head, throwing the crumpled mask to the ground.

He reached Igor, Boris and Katrina.

The Russian lovely ran into his arms for one hell of a hug and kiss that did not take long but said plenty.

He set her down with a grin. "Glad to see you, too," he told the three of them.

Igor looked up the road in the direction of the base. "Here they come!" he snarled. "A jeepful of the bastards!"

They hurried toward the truck.

Bolan and Katrina ran holding hands.

"My prayers have been answered," she told Bolan breathlessly as they reached the truck. "I thought I would never see you again!"

He took the truck's steering wheel. "Thanks for the pickup," he told Katrina as she flopped into the seat alongside him.

"I told my friends what you did for me, what you did for all of us," she said as he cranked the ignition to life. "I told the different cell leaders that we must combine forces to get you out. We are stronger now. Niktov's people told us what the objective was, and we came here to help."

Igor and Boris rushed to the back of the truck. They opened the rear doors and hopped in.

Bolan slammed the truck into forward motion.

The military vehicle full of KGB pursuers was closing in fast, less than a tenth of a kilometer behind them.

Bolan had tried to demolish all of the Balashika vehicles with his strafing run back at the base but obviously had missed this one. Now it was filled with eight savages, almost upon them.

He fed the truck all it had, upshifting, gaining some speed, but not enough. He looked at the rearview mirror.

He saw Igor holding open the rear doors of the truck for Boris, who aimed and fired a rifle grenade launcher, which resounded loudly within the confines of the truck. An instant later the pursuing vehicle exploded into a twisting, turning, rolling ball of fire and airborne bodies, the sound of the blast lost to Bolan beneath the whine of the truck's engine.

They hurtled down the highway toward the suburbs of Moscow where they could lose themselves in heavy traffic.

Bolan, steering the truck with a good woman named Katrina sitting beside him, felt a mixture of sensations. He felt satisfaction at a mission that was now smoldering evidence of a job well done. A worldwide terror machine without the powers that had ruled it for so long would be replaced by the chaos such a vacuum always brings. And a dissident movement within Russia would be made stronger than ever before as Katrina herself had told Bolan.

A blood debt had been settled.

There could be no doubt this time. Strakhov had slipped through Bolan's fingers, but he would never again lift a finger to order atrocities and horror.

A woman named April Rose could rest easy; a large-living soul set free now that those who had master-minded her death had been taken care of. And an Executioner named Bolan could maybe afford himself a short respite from hell.

Another large-living soul named Katrina had already touched him where it counted. Where a man needs to be touched, in the heart and mind and spirit, to remind him that he is a man; that the miles through hell on earth mean something, are worth the sacrifice.

He needed this woman. He could see in her eyes that she needed him in that same way. Those "better circumstances" he had mentioned to her two hours ago were finally at hand and those moments to come, shared with Katrina, stolen from everything else, would mean something, too.

Maybe he would forget a two-timing bitch named Tanya.

The bottom line was that the mission objective had been achieved.

The KGB high command was in ruins.

Strakhov was dead.

April Rose would rest in peace....

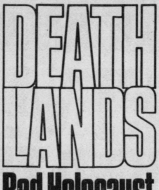

TAKE 'EM NOW

FOLDING SUNGLASSES
FROM GOLD EAGLE

Mean up your act with these tough, street-smart shades. Practical, too, because they fold 3 times into a handy, zip-up polyurethane pouch that fits neatly into your pocket. Rugged metal frame. Scratch-resistant acrylic lenses. Best of all, they can be yours for only $6.99. **MAIL ORDER TODAY.**

Send your name, address, and zip code, along with a check or money order for just $6.99 + .75¢ for postage and handling (for a total of $7.74) payable to Gold Eagle Reader Service, a division of Worldwide Library. New York and Arizona residents please add applicable sales tax.

Remove from pouch...

unfold once...

unfold twice...

and they're ready to wear.

GOLD EAGLE Gold Eagle Reader Service
901 Fuhrmann Blvd.
P.O. Box 1325
Buffalo, N.Y. 14240-1325

GES1–RRR

Offer not available in Canada.